KINDRED SPIRITS

BETTINA M. JOHNSON

Aqua Raven Publishing

Kindred Spirits

ISBN: 978-1-7365176-4-2 (paperback)

Cover art by Tina Adams

PROLOGUE

If I can't have her, no one can. Isn't that what every villain says? Only in my case, I'm not the villain. I truly love her. She will be mine, and I will use the positive energy I am putting out in the universe to get what I want—Margaret Fortune.

She calls herself Maggie—they all do, but I don't believe in nicknames. She will come around. I have my ways.

I followed her to the hair salon. Only she didn't see me. I'm a shadow. The man of her dreams—and she will dream about me. I have magic at my disposal. Anyone who gets in my way will have to be eliminated, of course.

All is fair in love and war.

This is war. To the victor go the spoils. Margaret will see this once I show her by each victory I achieve.

I don't have to tell her I stacked the deck in my favor. She needn't know any of the details. She's just a woman. They only think they deserve the truth and nothing but the truth. But in reality, women only need enough to keep them happy...and that means serving her man and keeping the house tidy.

Oh, once I make her my wife, she will never leave the house again. No job for her. A woman's place is in the home.

Margaret will come to learn her place.
She has no choice.
She never did.

CHAPTER 1

"We're heading down to Georgia with a banjo on our knee!"

"Ugh! Make it stop. Please, make it stop!" I cried. "You're killing me."

My sister Ellie had been singing ridiculous nonsensical words to old folk songs since we departed from Mystic Valley, North Carolina and our homestead, with our caravan of antique appraisers and dealers. We were heading to Sweet Briar, Georgia to meet up with our cousins and spend a week at the new fairgrounds where we'd set up our tents and wheel and deal in the wonderful world of priceless antiques and unique junk.

This was our livelihood if you didn't count our secret occupation as monster-hunters. You heard me right. Ellie, me, and my entire gang of nine other paranormals had a side job where anything and everything malevolent would be hunted down and eradicated before harm could befall innocents.

"Oh, pooh! The only thing around here that've been killed are those poor, innocent, smushed bugs on your windshield. RVs and insects do NOT mix," said Ellie with a shudder.

That was an entirely different kind of innocent.

I usually meant the human race when I referred to those naïve in the fact that the things that go bump in the night were not imaginary made-up monsters you joked about around a campfire. Most of the evil in our paranormal world preyed upon the innocuous humans. Although we've had to expunge a few humans off this planet a time or two when we'd come up against an insane serial killer or person with murderous intent—they might be innocents compared to paranormal beings, but some of them were hardly pure!

All you had to do was watch the news.

FOR THE MOST PART, my gang spent most of their time appraising the odd and unusual in the antique world by day, and the rest of the time taking out a renegade witch, a rabid werewolf, rampaging pixies, or slobbering trolls who explode when anxious. No, really. We even had a case once where fifteen young vampires became enamored of Anne Rice's tale and thought it a good idea to recreate *Interview with A Vampire*—on Staten Island instead of New Orleans.

That was a freak show of epic proportions. Do you have *any* idea how many freaky human kids are running around all goth on that island? It took us three weeks to distinguish the renegades from the degenerate unwashed teens running amok with fake pointy teeth then round them up. It was a nightmare!

"Fine. Ninety-nine bottles of shine on the wall, ninety-nine bottles of shine, take one down and pass it around, you can have yours, I'll have mine! Moonshine, that is!"

Ellie sang loud and proud, knowing I was the only one who could bear witness to her off-key torture.

Why?

My sister is a ghost. Yep. She is dearly departed but not gone from this realm and is the eleventh honorary member of the monster-fighting team. Every member of our team can see Ellie, but I am the only one who can hear her. Although after a recent interaction with a vampire most everyone who knows her can now hear her too. It's a long, sordid, and tragic tale, but Ellie was murdered by a man who attacked her trying to retrieve a wolf figurine he'd left to be appraised. We don't know why he did or what he wanted from us or Ellie, but the weird thing is, after she died, her body would not decompose.

She looked like Snow White—beautiful, cold, very much dead but in a sleeping state. Once we realized the situation, my family had Ellie encased in a glass coffin and her body is now residing in my Aunt Morwena's climate-controlled basement. However, a recent collaboration with a friendly vampire had Ellie's ghost days numbered—or so we hoped. Caliente Saunders, the vamp in question, managed to reverse a bit of the dark magic surrounding Ellie, and now everyone on my team can see AND hear her—including my father, which came as quite a shock.

Yeah, it was odd.

But then again, my entire family is odd. Witches, some of us psychic, a few of us insane—OK, I might have made that last one up. But sometimes it seems that way. I mean, I currently have a loopy ghost twin serenading me with road trip tunes, singing off-key and laughing maniacally.

You try telling me insanity doesn't run in my family.

My name is Maggie Fortune, witch, psychic, and appraiser of all the weird and wonderful that come into my tent. I also happen to be the leader of the United States delegation of the Biodag. The law of our land—although the team doesn't have a name, so secret is our organization. The Order of Origin is the head of the paranormal world and makes all the rules and regulations we in the Breed—what we call ourselves to distinguish us from humans—must abide by. Not only do I keep the fact that I am the leader a secret from my people, but I also pretend my second in command, Antoine, is the head of our merry band of mischief-makers. Easier that the tall, dark, and handsome vampire be the figurehead and I remain in the background.

I chose this because my family owns the antique business, and is very powerful, very wealthy, and I refuse to have those in my charge believe I got my title because Dear Old Dad bought my position. I've worked very hard to get where I am, and I want to prove myself through action and deed before the members of my team pass judgment. Someday they will find out, I'm sure. But right now, I can enjoy being "one of the guys."

Ellie thinks I'm crazy for hiding behind Antoine's capable leadership role. But what does she know? I was born a full ten minutes before my raven-haired sibling, and I never let her forget it. Not identical twins, for I'm a flaming redhead, we constantly bicker over who is the smartest, or prettiest, or what have you. But despite this, we love each other dearly, and not a day goes by when I don't fret that we haven't spent enough time trying to find the man who killed my sister and brought him to justice.

Something I intend to rectify very shortly if Caliente is to be believed!

"You are giving me a headache!" I switched on the satellite radio in the hopes Ellie'd listen to music rather than belt it out.

"Somebody is still upset about Daniel Grayson making

moony-eyes at her. I told you I'm sorry I put the suggestion you were still infatuated with him in his mind. I had to think quick and that's the first thing that popped in my mind," said Ellie.

I'd recently had the unfortunate happen. My old boyfriend came back into the picture when a murder occurred at my family compound—he is a police investigator. We'd parted a long time ago after he thought he'd "knocked me up," as Ellie once put it, but it turned out to be a false alarm. I've never forgiven him for being the type of guy to cut his losses and run from responsibility. Now that we are all grown up he seems to want to let bygones be bygones, especially since Ellie used her magical powers of suggestion to distract the man from looking too carefully at the case we'd solved and altered to protect my "special" group. Only Ellie put the idea in his mind that I still liked him.

As if.

"I'm not upset about that." A lie.

I put my signal on and changed lanes, cringing when Ellie began to hum along with a song. I knew she'd start caterwauling any minute now.

"Plus, who told you to give my cell number to Garrison Black? He's been bugging me with sales and appraisal questions that are best left with Estelle and her two assistants!"

I left the main antique business in the capable hands of my father's trusted human manager, Estelle Longo. Her two assistants, Sandy and Cassie Booker usually dealt with our human workers and any questions and issues that came up.

"I didn't give it to Dad. He probably told Garrison by accident if someone gave it to him. You know Dad, quickly passing the buck to one of his underlings—in this case, us

—so he can spend all his time jet-setting around the world with one of his tramps."

Ellie was not a fan of my father and his playboy life-style. Even since my mom passed away from cancer, dad has been burying his sorrow in excess—and that includes women. Or so said my Aunt Morwena. I think Dad is afraid of dying, so he is living large rather than dealing with middle age. And when you consider my dad is a witch like the rest of my family, he hasn't even reached the middle of his life yet, nor would he until he's about seventy-five or so. My father is fifty-six.

Yeah.

Just then Ellie switched from humming to all-out singing, and even my cat, Bob, was over it. He scooted into the back bedroom area with a swish of his tail.

"If you don't stop I will find an oldies station and blast Barry Manilow or someone and ruin your mood," I warned, grabbing a handful of the Skittles I was munching on and shoving them in my mouth.

"I love Barry! 'I write the songs that make the whole world swing, I write the songs of lust and all kinky things!' " Ellie trailed off with a fit of giggles that ended in a snort.

Sigh.

Are we there yet?

CHAPTER 2

"Have you noticed that dark sedan stays about two car lengths behind us and never lets another car move in front of his?" Ellie asked an hour later.

"What? No. Which one?" I looked out my side mirrors and didn't detect any dark sedan. But just then, a minivan moved one lane over, and there it was. "He's been following us?"

"I think so. Let me go find out what's up."

Before I could stop her, Ellie whisked out of my RV and went to check out the mystery driver...or so I assumed. This might seem odd, but since my sister *is* a ghost, floating out of one vehicle and over into another was a piece of cake. I'm getting better at not fretting over her disappearing acts or daring exploits—it's not like much can harm her. Not anymore. Although, since Ellie is not a traditional ghost, but could very well have the dark spell that turned her into a spook reversed, my anxiety that something will happen to her before my cousin Lily and some of the extended family of witches can work on bringing her back has tripled.

That was one of the reasons we were heading back to Sweet Briar, Georgia. To pay a visit to my Croy relations—which extends to Lily's family of Sweets and Dolces. (Yes, I know Dolce means Sweet in Italian. It's a long story, but someone in the past Americanized the name). The other reason is my paranormal crew of antique appraisers is setting up camp at the new fairgrounds in town that is the backdrop for a permanent craft fair where artisans have booths and tents with a larger indoor building perfect for antique auctions and the like.

My smaller delegation of dealers—those that deal in the outré and unusual that caters to the magical world—will remain in the visitor's outdoor section, while my father's traditional antique faction will take over the indoor spot. We will be visiting for a week, and I can't wait to see Lily again.

"He seems like a boring dude singing along to Coldplay and picking his nose." Ellie came popping back in and sat next to me as I continued down Highway 64.

"Does it look like he's following us specifically, or is it a coincidence that he's been with us all this time?"

"Not sure. He does have luggage in the back, and it looks like boxes in his trunk. Maybe he's a traveling salesman and we happen to be heading along the same route. It's not as if there are many roads to choose from going from our part of North Carolina to Georgia!"

True.

I tried to shrug off the feeling that we were being watched—or followed, as it were—and get back to relaxed yet annoyed with Ellie for her lousy singing and lyric assassination attempts. After about fifteen minutes of constantly staring out the window to check my mirrors, I punched in the number of the one person who always managed to calm me down when my Spidey sense kicked in.

"Boss," Antoine was a man of few words. Er, vampire, that is.

"That's you about six vehicles back right? You have me in your sights?"

"I do."

"Have you noticed anything unusual while driving? Not glaringly obvious, but something that made you pay attention or keep watch?"

I could hear Antoine sigh and deliberate how he would answer my cryptic questions. When another thirty seconds went by with no response, I almost checked my phone to see if our line dropped. But then he began to speak. "A dark sedan has been staying two to three cars behind you and has since we got on the highway an hour ago. But Mags, it's not like we are on a massive interstate. We are on a small country highway in the mountains and perhaps this person is heading to Georgia, same as us."

"I know, but I kind of hoped he would have stayed on Highway 64 when we hit Franklin, but he followed us onto Highway 23 and we are almost to the border. Maybe it's nothing, and I'm just jittery."

"Don't borrow trouble. It finds you no matter. Let's stay alert and see what comes of it."

"Roger."

"I'll keep watch. And Mags?"

"Yeah?"

"Don't call me Roger." Antoine chuckled and disconnected. His brevity lightened my mood and the knowledge that a full-blooded vampire was guarding my back eased some of the tension I'd been feeling since Ellie mentioned the car possibly tailing us.

My team was ambling down the highway, we were a day behind the main antique operation that had arrived at our destination yesterday. A few of us shared living quarters in RVs and towed our vehicles behind them. Although some of us lived solo, as was my case—unless you considered Ellie.

"Hey, girlie. Sorry I slept." Bella, our group's earth elemental, and perpetual teenage soul came stumbling out of my bedroom where she'd been dead to the world for most of the trip. Bella usually rode with Dara, our druidic cleric, but decided to keep me company since Dara banned her from their RV. The reason behind Bella's exile was partly due to the fact Dara kept her *Learn French in 100 Days* tapes playing incessantly, and it drove Bella to distraction so badly she began speaking in multiple languages to keep things lively. Dara did not appreciate this behavior, hence my temporary travel companion.

"We there yet, Mom? I'm bored!"

"Bella, go sit down and strap yourself in before I stop short and you go through the windshield," I scolded.

"We did that already! Remember Vegas? Fun times."

Bella had an odd sense of humor, and thankfully, pain didn't affect her like it did many paranormal beings. That trip had us running afoul of a werewolf biker pack and one of the wolves decided he didn't like the way Johnny, *my* team's werewolf, was sniffing around one of their females. Needless to say, it caused quite the fracas—but we came out on top. We always did. It's one of the reasons we did what we did for the Order of Origin—after all, they are the CIA of the paranormal world. They can't afford to have us be a bunch of puny fighters now, can they?

"You were picking glass out of your forehead for weeks." I smiled at the memory. I know. We're weird.

"Welcome to Georgia! Hey, we're here. What is it? Another fifteen minutes to Sweet Briar, give or take?" Bella began bouncing in the passenger seat Ellie had vacated and Bob, my tuxedo cat gave her an annoying "meow" from his post in my tiny kitchen area's sink. Bella could get on anyone's nerves if they weren't partial to bubbly enthusiasm and teenaged angst. That she was somewhere in her thousandth year didn't matter in the slightest. Bella looked and acted sixteen and used it to her advantage to ensnare those who tended to prey on nubile young things—and her track record was impressive.

"Give or take depending on how slowly we progress and any slow-moving tractors we come upon." The road to Sweet Briar is a two-way country lane and we have a team of RVs moving in formation to get to those fairgrounds. I just hope the event organizers remembered my smaller team was arriving today. Did Nathara get with Estelle and make sure all is well?"

Nathara, a dark witch, and all-around pain in my behind, was the coordinator for our group and did liaisons with the non-magical side. It was Estelle and Nathara's job to make sure each town we visited was ready for us and all the logistics were in order. Estelle, recently widowed when her husband, Dale, was murdered by a deranged ancient vampire-like being called a strix, had just come back from an extra week off where she'd been staying with family and settling Dale's estate.

The strix had been a creature from Bella's past and had kidnapped her baby sister eons ago. Not only did we recover her now-grown sister, Halona, we eradicated the evil woman and avenged Dale's murder in the process. Our little tribe took a hit, but we came together to support Estelle, and although damaged, we weren't broken—not by a long shot.

"Maybe there will be some cute men to flirt with in this town. Didn't you tell me the male witches were exceptionally hot in Sweet Briar when you came back from your short trip a few months back?"

"Never you mind how "hot" the men are. We have a job to do and I, for one, am sick of men," I grumped.

"You're still upset because Detective Daniel Grayson has been texting and calling you like a lovesick puppy," snickered Bella.

"Don't remind me."

Ellie had inadvertently placed a "suggestion" in the mind of one Daniel to remove the suspicions he'd been having during the strix fiasco. Only now, he was convinced we were soul mates and I wanted him back. I most assuredly did not. Ellie can't seem to get him to forget her prompting and surmises because he's always wanted me, even after he dumped me, so her power of suggestion isn't having the desired effect any longer. Seeing as I'm on the road most of the year, it won't be too much of a problem. But when we get back to Mystic Valley, North Carolina? Yeah.

Especially since things were heating up, albeit slowly, between me and a certain half-sorcerer, half-vampire Scotsman. Only now I'm wondering if Torquil MacDonald—Tor, for short—still had any desire to pick up where we'd left off. Which wasn't much of anything since Daniel ruined our first official date. We hadn't had a chance since, nor did it seem Tor was interested in me anymore if his aloofness had anything to do with it.

I'd already made the decision that I was in Sweet Briar to work, hang with my cousin Lily, and hopefully get some counsel on Ellie's ghostly condition. I had no time for men or dating.

None at all.

And I was going to keep telling myself that until I believed it.

"All clear, Mags!" Ellie drifted back to the front where Bella and I sat. "That car kept going straight and didn't follow us when we turned towards Sweet Briar...so I guess I was suspicious for nothing!"

"Someone was following us?" asked Bella.

"Apparently not. But for a while there, it looked like some guy in a dark sedan was doing just that," I said.

"Are you sure it isn't Daniel Grayson?" Bella chuckled then ducked when I tossed one of my Skittles at her head, but still managed to catch it in her mouth. Then both Bella and Ellie erupted in a fit of giggles.

Sigh.

I, for one, was glad we had arrived at our destination. Now I could only hope this would remain one, nice, uneventful stay despite the giggling duo.

CHAPTER 3

"This is the nicest fairground I've even been to!" gushed Ellie and she floated off to roam among the throngs of people shopping and playing in the warm June morning.

"It's one of the bigger ones we've encountered in such a small town like Sweet Briar, but it still can't compete with the big city fairs. Still, I'm impressed," I said, and Bella nodded in agreement. She could now hear Ellie as well as see her, because of that magic Caliente performed, as mentioned, so I wasn't the only one who both saw and heard my spooky sibling.

The decision to head back to Sweet Briar, Georgia was two-fold. Check out the new fairground since it has a terrific setup for an indoor and outdoor antique show, but also to meet up with Lily's great-grandmother on her father's side—no relation to me or Ellie—to seek her advice on the dark magic that made my sister a transparent entity that often cried, "boo!" just to keep up with appearances.

Even though Adriana Dolce wasn't a blood relation to my Fortune and Croy side, our families had always been close. And with Lily's father, Charlie, secretly marrying one of our Croy women, Lily's mother, Adelaide, it brought our combined families closer. It was quite a long and sordid tale, but Lily had recently brought her long-lost father home, much to the shock of everyone who had written the decades gone Charlie Sweet a lost cause. Compound this with the fact that none of us in the extended family knew the truth behind the secret marriage of Charlie and Adelaide. Yeah, the grapevine has been buzzing. I barely remembered the man, or Adelaide for that matter, so this would be new territory for me, and Ellie too.

"Oh, look! Here comes my cousin Lily and that's her fiancé, Lorcan, and her cousin Andrea." I waved in their direction even though they'd already spied me in the crowd. We wouldn't be doing our appraisals until tomorrow, so today was going to be spent meeting, greeting relations, and enjoying a massive family meal at my cousin Iona and her husband Owen's house—the only place large enough to host my party and all the relations that would be present. Iona was Lily's aunt, her mother Adelaide's eldest sister and my father, William's first cousin.

Yeah. Keeping everyone straight was already giving me a headache!

"Hey, stranger! How was the trip down to Georgia?" Lily asked then gave me a tentative embrace. Lily didn't seem like much of a hugger, and I respected her need for space, so I didn't cling onto her and force the hug to go on longer than she intended.

"It was uneventful, which a good thing with my group. Lily, this is my friend and associate, Bella. Bella this is my cousin Lily. And this is Lorcan Reid and Andrea Becker."

"Nice to meet you, Bella." I could see Lily was curious as to why I didn't mention Bella's surname. But elementals rarely shared that information with anyone outside their trusted people, and I'd leave it to her to correct my omission.

She didn't, so I suspected she'd hold her cards close for now.

"Where's Ellie? Is it really true everyone in your team can see and hear her now?"

"Yeah, that Caliente Saunders is some talented vamp...uh...wait. Are we supposed to be speaking out loud like this with all these tourists running around?" I asked worriedly.

"Don't sweat it," said Andrea. "We have a glamour over the entire village. When human tourists and non-magical residents not in our trusted group hear us talking about anything arcane, they hear something completely inane, so we can speak freely!"

Hmm...that would take some getting used to.

"Neat trick," said Bella, "And why we haven't employed this with the work we do is beyond me!"

"Something to discuss at our next meeting." I gave the earth elemental a fond smile. "I will inform our illustrious leader, Antoine."

Bella gave me an appraising look and I gulped inwardly that my secret might not be so secret as I'd hoped.

"When will we get to meet the rest of your team? Tonight?" Lily asked, looking around as if expecting to see a few vampires, a werewolf, a shifter, and the rest would pop out and yell "surprise" any minute now.

"Everyone is still settling in. They know dinner is at six sharp, and trust me, no one wants to miss a meal at one of the famous Dolce/Croy gatherings."

"Don't tell that to my Uncle Owen. He's a Haywood and is still sore my Aunt Iona goes by Croy-Haywood and not his surname alone!" cried Lily. "Speaking of which, it was decided my house is going to be our meeting place. Iona and Owen had an unexpected water main break, and other than the great-grandparents Victorian, my house is the only one that can accommodate a huge dinner party. Trust me...I'm used to hosting a crowd. It seems to happen on a regular basis!"

Just then, Ellie rushed up in a ghostly swirl of ectoplasm then squealed when she spied our cousin Lily.

"Lily! Hi. Oh, hey...so I'd love to be polite and all, but right now I have something urgent to tell my sister." Turning to me, Ellie tried to calm herself and not stream her words together in a mishmash of excitable nonsense as she was wont to do when distracted.

"I saw him again! That man! The one we thought was following your RV. I just saw him speaking to a vendor on the far side of the fairgrounds. What are the odds he'd be here after continuing straight earlier? Should we tell Antoine and have him check the guy out?"

"Someone was following you?" Lily and her friends looked concerned, so I tried to downplay it.

"Oh, I am sure it's nothing. His vehicle trailed us from our neck of the woods all the way to Dillard, Georgia where we turned to head here but he continued down to Clayton—or so we assumed. I guess he decided to come to the fairgrounds. I'm sure it's nothing.

Lily squinted in the direction Ellie had pointed and I could see her take a step in that direction, then stop herself.

A look passed between her and Lorcan and I wondered if things were still unsettled since her father's return, or if she was just being cautious.

"There's Brian Chase. How about we point out this man to him? He's a detective and can check things out for us then report back if there is anything to worry about," stated Lorcan.

"Good idea. I better go with Ellie since I'm not one-hundred-percent certain every paranormal out there can see and hear her yet. And she's the only one who knows what the guy looks like."

After introductions and a short explanation, it was decided we'd all head in the direction of the mystery man and follow closely behind Brian yet remain somewhat hidden to catch a glimpse. Perhaps it was nothing but coincidence. However, in my line of work, we didn't often believe in them much! Our skepticism has never let us down—and more often than not, kept us alive and well!

"Is that him there?" Bella asked, looking to where Ellie had led Brian Chase.

It obviously was since Brian began engaging the man in conversation.

"He looks awfully familiar, doesn't he, Lily?" Andrea tilted her head as if gazing at the two men sideways would give her a better viewpoint.

"That's because he looks so much like Dev Patel. They could be twins!" she responded. Lily went on to explain that Dev was the local veterinary assistant, and her observation was backed up when the man himself rushed over to greet our mysterious stranger. "Well, that clears things up. Dev obviously knows this person—and is more than likely related. So, I don't think we are dealing with anything untoward," she said.

I certainly wanted Lily to be correct. I was ready for

some rest, relaxation, good times with loved ones, and a profitable week doing nothing more than appraisals—and a bit of dabbling in dark magic to bring my sister back from the great beyond!

I hoped.

CHAPTER 4

"**A**re you sure it's OK to bring Bob with us? I've heard some things about Lily's cat, Wicked, and I don't want Bob to wind up in the kitty ER," Ellie asked worriedly.

"Lily said Wicked promised to be on her best behavior. Although how she knows her cat promised such a thing is beyond me. Let's bring him in and if things go south, we can keep him in his carrier. I just hope we have extra kibble, or he'll get surly," I said.

We would be a lively group tonight with the omission of the two people I was most curious about—Charlie and Adelaide Sweet. It seemed that a few days after Charlie's return, he took ill—something to do with the dark magic that he's had in him for decades. He was at a witch's retreat, sort of a mental health facility combined with dark magic detox spa, where he and Adelaide were seeking out the help he needed to heal and rejoin proper witch society. Lily was still dealing with the fact that her long-lost father was gone again, but I thought she was holding up well, all things considered.

That left my cousin Iona, Lily's aunt, as the only Croy in attendance along with Owen, her spouse. Adriana Dolce would be there as well as her granddaughter Chiara, Charlie Sweet's sister, and Andrea's mother. Chiara's husband Stephen and stepson Steve Junior and Lorcan's parents, Eileen and Henry, were longtime friends of ours, and Ellie was excited to find out if they would be able to see and hear her since the last time we'd gotten together she'd been isolated in her spirit form.

Lily's friend Jake and girlfriend Becky were coming, and so were Jake's parents, June and Dennis Carter—more friends we'd known for years. This time around, they'd get to meet my team of paranormal monster-hunters and I'd get to meet someone Lily called Pandora. The fact that she glanced nervously at Andrea when she'd mentioned her had my curiosity piqued.

"I always make sure you packed extra kibble for Bob. It doesn't stop him from complaining loudly when he eats that as well as his usual portion in five minutes then has nothing until we head back home," Ellie complained.

Bob was a rather rotund tuxedo feline and no manner of diets or restricting his food intake seemed to work. The boy could eat!

"I'm sure Lily will let us have a bit of Wicked's food if...whoa! Who is *that?*"

I'd just turned my old Grand Wagoneer into Lily's gravel drive and spied a leggy blonde in an over-the-top outfit straight out of Frederick's of Hollywood. If you've never heard of the place, think Victoria's Secret on acid.

"Is that young lady wearing lingerie in public?" Dara asked. Her rosy cheeks turned a darker shade of red as she quickly pulled her unruly mane of curly brown hair streaked with grey into a ponytail. "I mean, I'm no prude, but that's a thong!"

"Um, it's more like dental floss," said Bella with a frown.

Uh oh.

I didn't want this to spiral out of control in a hurry, especially since close on my heels would be the arrival of some of the male delegation from my team.

We'd just parked and climbed out of my vehicle when cousin Lily came slamming out the side door of her home.

"Pandora! What do you think you are doing? Get in the house and put on something decent before you shock someone into cardiac arrest!"

"You told me this would be an informal and easy evening and to dress in something comfortable!" The stunning blonde, who I now knew was the character Lily mentioned we'd be meeting tonight, tossed her hair behind one shoulder and pouted.

"So that means taking off most of your clothing and putting on strings and gauze pads?" Lily, hands on hips, had an exasperated look on her face that made me think this kind of thing happened regularly with Pandora.

"Hey! I was going to go crotchless, but I managed to stop myself even though that is my definition of comfortable." Pandora turned to us and smiled in welcome. I think I was the only one who smiled back. Pandora then performed a hand wiggle motion and suddenly wore tight jean shorts and a *barely-there* tee that had her midriff showing. "Hi, folks. I'm Dorie!"

"Hi, Dor..." I started.

"That's hardly an improvement. You aren't wearing a bra!" Lily continued to argue.

"I'm not wearing any underwear now either, sugar. You have to pick your battles!"

Lily gave us a grimace of a smile and began to apologize.

"Don't mind Dorie. She's a bit of a wild spirit and likes attention. We..."

"That's no wild spirit," interrupted Bella who been staring daggers at the blonde woman, "That's a crossroads demon."

Before I knew what happened, Bella had the ground rumbling around us, and a shimmering vine-like substance began oozing from her fingertips. I knew in a matter of minutes my feisty elemental would have Lily's friend hogtied and at her mercy if I didn't do something—and quick.

"Bella..."

Before I could utter another word, Pandora chuckled and pointed one finger in Bella's direction, then turned and walked into Lily's house.

Bella remained standing rooted to the spot, but where her magic had been coiling out and weaving toward the demon, only a dangling string of yarn remained—and the earth stopped trembling.

Eek.

Pandora made Bella seem like an apprentice all wet behind the ears and not the ancient being she truly was. What the heck is a crossroads demon anyway? Weren't they those imps that hung out on dead-end streets or something? I didn't think that meant they would be super powerful beings! Lily had some explaining to do.

I followed my cousin as she invited us into her home when another thought crossed my mind—this one making me jolt in shock and instantly become anxious. If Bella was suspicious of this crossroads demon, what would Serena and Sydney, our pair of weapons-master succubi do when they got ahold of her? Pandora might have their demonic Breed in common with my succubae partners, but even I knew they were not cut from the same cloth.

Things were about to get interesting.

§⌖

"So isn't this neat? You can all see and hear Ellie. Why didn't you tell me you knew Caliente, Mortimer and Valgaard? Such a big help last week—all three of them. Can you pass the salad?" I was rambling while tossing nervous glances between Pandora, who was stuffing her third pepperoni pizza into her mouth—yes, that's pizza, not slice—and Serena, Sydney, and Bella who were standing in a corner of Lily's living room and hissing.

Just after our last case where Bella transformed from a sixteen-year-old-looking bubble gum-popping nuisance into a bronzed goddess of earth magic fury, Serena and Sydney had been having a friendly pecking-order-like competition with her to reestablish their big, bad status. Now it looks like the three banded together against a common enemy—a pizza-eating gluttonous one.

I widened my eyes at the trio and rolled my lips into my mouth trying to get their attention, shaking my head and slightly nodding toward the other end of the table where they should be sitting and enjoying food. The women remained rooted to the spot and chose to ignore me.

This was not going as I envisioned.

"More tea? Soda? Does anyone want a beer?" Lily gulped out.

If having the prickly demons and an irate elemental weren't enough, the men in my team had suddenly morphed into pre-pubescent teenaged boys who just had a life-sized pinup model come out of their girlie magazine and materialize in their world. In other words, they were drooling—hooting and howling would follow, I'm sure of it. Even Antoine had a bemused look cross his face every time his eyes landed on Pandora—which was often. He was sitting beside Dara who kept trying to distract him with small talk.

If that wasn't bad enough, the meeting of felines did *not* go well. Right now, Bob was sequestered in his cage, while an irate Wicked paced back and forth in front of it occasionally arching her back and hissing. The growling was getting on everyone's nerves.

Only Nathara seemed unphased and continued to munch on her salad, regaling the room with our latest exploits—which had us rescuing Bella's younger sister and defeating that strix I'd mentioned. Since no one was contradicting her, Nathara was making herself out to be the heroine. Lorcan and Jake's parents were the only ones paying her any mind, nodding their heads and making the appropriate noises all the while casting nervous glances at my people...and the cats!

"OK, that's it. Pandora, if you touch another pizza, I will turn you back into a book. You three, come over here and sit down before I get mad enough to turn *you* into those three trolls that were solidified into stone in The Hobbit." Adriana Dolce, formidable dark witch and a tiny ancient version of what Lily would assuredly look like in a hundred years or so, stood up and scolded the recalcitrant trio and the crossroads demon.

Pandora burped—loudly—then blinked slowly and smiled. She'd managed to pour most of her water down the front of her top earlier, and it was white—and see-through. Now putting on an air of innocence was a farce in the making considering her top left nothing to the imagination in its wet condition.

"I'm sorry, Is there something wrong?"

An understatement if I ever heard one.

"Oh, there is something wrong all right," said Bella,

marching into the dining room. "Why is there a crossroads demon here and just what were you thinking in befriending it?"

Wow. I'd never seen Bella this riled up. And *it?* That was downright rude.

"What's wrong with a crossroads demon?" Ellie asked, perplexed, yet still flush with excitement that everyone present could see and hear her. It caused Lily's resident ghost, one Edith Plank, to become jealous enough with everyone making a fuss over Ellie that she'd departed in a swirl of indignant ectoplasm. "Aren't they minor demons who stand around crossroads at midnight and make bargains with desperate victims who'd give up their soul for luxury and wealth and the like?"

"Minor? Oh, sugar...there is nothing *minor* about me," Dorie chuckled darkly.

"That's it. Let's go outside, you puffed up imp. I will show you who the better demon is," shouted Sydney while strutting to the table with a menacing glare on her face.

Serena came charging over to the table behind her and placed her hands down upon it, leaning forward slightly. "Yes, stop making such a gluttonous pig of yourself and show us what you've got. Unless you are too afraid?"

Since I'd never witnessed the two succubi looking the slightest bit flustered, even in the middle of an epic battle, I sucked in air so fast I began to cough and sputter.

"I'm afraid? The two of you against little old me makes it seem like y'all know you'd be on the losing end of that brawl," Pandora sighed. "Children, children. Do they teach you nothing in fire and brimstone academy? There is nothing stronger than a crossroads demon once she's flipped her switch, and you're making me cranky. Now shoo!"

Both succubi raised themselves up in outrage and Bella started having facial tics.

"That's it. You're toast!" Bella shouted.

I felt a fissure go through the room and my ears had a popping sensation almost akin to being thousands of feet up in an airplane. I blinked a few times when it felt like a gentle mist passed over my skin, then I looked around.

Nothing was the same as it was only seconds earlier. *Nothing.*

The place where Pandora had been sitting was now devoid of the crossroads demon who was lounging on the loveseat in the living room twiddling her thumbs. Sydney, Serena, and Bella were standing in the dining room in exactly the same spots they'd been in, only they didn't have any clothing on except for underwear—their articles of clothing were strung above the table from one end of the ceiling to the other on what looked to be an old plastic clothesline cord.

Adriana Dolce remained rooted in place, her hand in the air like she'd been scolding prior to whatever this was, only now she had chopsticks sticking out of her tightly wound bun and wore a garish shade of hot pink lipstick. She reached up to pull the chopsticks out of her hair, causing the bun to loosen and hair to come cascading down her shoulders. The chopsticks, fancy stainless steel ones, clattered to the table and I scooped them up and tucked them in my purse because if looks could kill, Adriana would surely be using them any second now!

Even the men didn't come out of this unscathed—they too wore the same shade of pink as Adriana. Sven, our shifter, had a telltale lipstick print on his face like he'd been kissed in passing.

Jake was sitting on Lorcan's lap, and Becky, Jake's girlfriend, was sitting on Andrea's. The older set hadn't been touched, yet all their drinks were replaced with tiny boxes of Yoo-hoo. Lily had a banana peel perched on top of her head.

I was the only one who hadn't been besmirched by the now guffawing crossroads demon. Maybe it was because I'd smiled at her earlier, but I just didn't know.

Ellie was hovering in the corner looking incredulous, and I'd have to query her as to whether or not she'd been affected by Pandora's display of power and trickery.

"If you folks are finished with your grandstanding, let's move on to dessert," suggested Dorie. "I'm starving!"

"Merooow!" screeched Wicked.

"Hiss!" replied Bob.

Sigh.

Somehow, I suspect this will turn out to be the longest week of my life.

CHAPTER 5

"This looks to be from the Civil War era. If I'm not mistaken, it's a brass button off a Northern soldier's uniform," I'd informed my seventh customer of the day. The man had a box of stuff he wanted me to look at, and I became disgruntled with Estelle for sending non-magical people to mine and Bella's tent. Were there no paranormals wanting an item looked over in this town?

"That would be the War of Northern Aggression, thank you. And if this here belongs to a Yankee, you can keep it." He glanced over at Bella then turned back to me and winked. "Your little partner over there looks like she's got some mixed blood in her. Shame what happened to our culture."

Let it go, man. I mean, really! What an idiot.

Reaching out and sighing his displeasure, he retrieved the coin and tucked it into his pocket. If he'd noticed my gloved hands on this warm June day, he chose not to mention it, but I caught his repeated glance. "Maybe I will go talk to that tall fella you got with all them hunting knives. I betcha he knows more about coins than a pretty little thing such as yourself."

When I didn't react, the man squinted in disbelief, threw one more look in Bella's direction, then stood. Hitching his paints up, he hawked out a bit of the tobacco he'd been chewing, picked up his box, and left my tent without a backward glance. Good riddance!

"I should animate that spittle and thwack it into the back of that clod's head," Bella sniffed.

"He isn't worth your energy. I wonder why we aren't getting any Breed coming in. It looks like the entire town has attracted nothing but human tourists. Not that I mind, per se, but I always hope for something a bit on the unusually spooky side, and we rarely find that with humans."

"Not true," said Bella. "All it will take is one of these tourists to come in here with a possessed doll and you'll change your tune in a hurry! What's with the chopsticks by the way?"

I forgot that I'd placed them in my purse for safe-keeping and had stuck them in my tip jar where they would remain until I could either give them to Lily or Adriana—I wasn't' sure to whom they really belonged! For all I knew, Pandora conjured them out of thin air!

We heard a soft cough and looked up guiltily that we might have been overheard by a non-magical being, but I groaned inwardly when I saw the man from yesterday hovering at the flap to our tent.

"Miss Fortune, I presume?" Levi Patel as we'd been informed his name was by that nice detective friend of Lily's, had hurriedly rushed over to apologize if his following so closely had alarmed us in any way. We'd been gracious and laughed off our paranoia, but now it seems I'd picked up an admirer. Levi had shown up no less than three times today asking if I needed anything and offering to show me his collection of odds and ends. While his wares were mildly curious in a strictly professional sense, his amorous advances were wearing thin.

I'd even had Johnny flash his werewolf at the guy and Garrison Black, the mild-mannered human appraiser on my dad's side of the business had even taken notice to the extent he'd come to my rescue once or twice escorting the lovesick witch away from me and back to his booth on the opposite side of the fairground from where we had our setup.

Estelle promised to contact his cousin, Dev Patel, the hapless veterinary assistant to have a talk with his kin and try to get him to understand these advances toward me were unwanted. If that didn't work, Estelle threatened to contact my father! Since I didn't want that, I knew I had to deal with this buffoon on my own.

"Mr. Patel. Was there something I can help you with?" Trying to keep it formal still had my face aching from the slight smile I had plastered on it—not that it seemed to get through to this lug nut.

"Well, seeing as how it is lunch time, and you now know from my glowing recommendation by my illustrious brother, Dev, that I am not a threat but a humble man with the same passions as yourself, perhaps you would honor me with a luncheon date?"

Is this dude for real?

"Oh! Well, listen, I'm sort of seeing..."

"And that lovely dark witch, Nathara, is it? She informed me you aren't dating anyone, so this looks like a wonderful way to get to know one another. Especially seeing as how you will be here all week and are related to Lily Sweet. You will be back and forth from North Carolina to Georgia often. It is kismet!"

It was hardly kismet, but I had a feeling my protestations wouldn't get through this one's thick skull.

I stood up and walked over to Levi then grabbed his elbow, leading him out of my tent to allow entry to a customer waiting on Bella. I could see Tor come out of his tent with the scowling man who'd been my last appraisal and from both their demeanors, I could tell things didn't go the way the client wanted.

"Mr. Patel..."

"Levi, please."

"Mr. Patel. I'm sorry, but I am otherwise occupied with a certain gentleman, and I don't think he'd be too pleased to see you hanging around me. As a matter of fact..."

Before I could finish my response, another figure loomed up on my right side and I felt myself swooped up into the arms of Daniel Grayson. "Sweetie pie! Fancy meeting you here! Are you working? Did you miss me?"

I opened my mouth in utter astonishment, and that was the very moment Detective Grayson decided it was perfectly fine to plant a sloppy, wet kiss on me. I was shocked. Levi looked crestfallen. And Tor? Tor looked like he wanted to rip someone's head off. I just wasn't sure if it was my two male admirers or my own head he was contemplating. The stoic look he gave me spoke volumes. So did the way he turned and stomped back into his tent.

Ugh. Why me? Why now?

Before I could react to that one kiss, Levi Patel drew himself up and pushed in between Danny and me. Turning to the detective, we voiced his displeasure by hauling off and throwing a punch in his direction. Daniel Grayson was no slacker, however, and easily sidestepped the swinging fist.

Turning to me in outrage, Levi leaned in and planted his own kiss on me before I knew what was happening. I countered this with a hard slap to his face and threats of death and dismemberment if he ever tried doing that again.

Half the tourists stared openmouthed at our antics, but I managed to garner a few catcalls and whistles. Estelle came running. Garrison gave me a look asking if I wanted him to step in—I quickly shook my head no, and Antoine loomed in the distance, his stride parting the sea of people having him reach us first.

Just great!

Could someone please tell me why my quiet week of rest and relaxation was turning into a Greek tragedy in the making?

"This cousin of yours certainly keeps interesting company." Johnny was watching Antoine grill steaks outside our collective RVs later that evening while Dara prepared the sides in our makeshift outdoor kitchen. The men had set up our picnic tables and benches and the women were helping with the setup and meal preparation. Fairly traditional roles, until one noticed Bella strutting by holding a keg in one hand and roller skates in the other. We parked the RVs strategically on the outskirts of the fairgrounds, so we had privacy in the evenings when we were finished with our appraisal duties.

"I can't wait until the rest of the tourists clear out. I plan on whizzing around these wonderful brick pathways at top speed!" she cried as she passed by where I was sitting.

"Pandora certainly is different," I replied.

"I mean, I know she is a demon and all, but so are Serena and Sydney. I don't understand why the sudden dislike among you women." Johnny stretched and each well-defined muscle rippled under his form-fitting shirt. He flashed me a wolfish grin to show me he was teasing. It still rankled.

Werewolves!

"Perhaps it was that uncalled for display of evil power she threw at us. Or the fact she acts like a strumpet and has the men dazzled by cheap parlor tricks and nudity!" Dara grumbled. Poor Dara had insisted on her non-prudish outlook, but she of everyone present, kept harping on the fact Pandora couldn't seem to keep her clothing on very long.

"It's the heat. When the heat turns up, it's my natural instinct to want to run around in my birthday suit!" she'd protested. None of us were much impressed by this excuse for bare skin. Well, none of us *women*, anyway. What's more, despite what Dara says, that was no display of cheap parlor tricks—Dorie was formidable.

"I'm surprised Nathara seems unbothered by Pandora. You'd think her insecurities would be running rampant about now and she'd ratchet up her sex appeal and glamour for all the men in a hundred-mile radius," said Ellie. Speaking of someone who didn't seem bothered by Pandora, Ellie had spent the morning hanging with the crossroads demon at Lily's home and had nothing but glowing things to say about her.

Ellie could make friends with anyone, however. I mean...part of the tragedy of her being a ghost was how extroverted she used to be. Life of the party, going hither and yon, always out and about, visiting and such, the irony that she was the one most people couldn't see or hear was a double-edged sword. Now me on the other hand? Give me a good mystery novel and the solitary life curled up in my RV with Bob, and I was perfectly content to go weeks without seeing anyone else. Bob might be more upset with the solitude than me—and he's a furball!

Speaking of Ellie...

"Did you and Adriana have a chat about what Caliente Saunders suggested? What did she have to say about trying to reverse your dark spell and bring you back among the living?" I asked my sister.

Ellie brightened considerably and informed me Adriana would consult with Caliente and a few of her witch friends and begin working on a few different counterspells to try out. "Adriana warned me not to expect results in a week, or even a few months. Apparently, the magic needed might be a long time coming. Lily seemed upset when Adriana mentioned a forbidden library or some such—I wonder why?" Ellie flitted around us like a butterfly in her excitement. "But Adriana did say she thought it only a matter of time and effort, and I will have my body back! Can you imagine?"

And now, with her grandson Charlie, Lily's father, home safe—well, recuperating in a hospital anyway—Adriana had that time to dedicate to Ellie's spell-reversal and subsequent return to normal. Or so I hoped.

"I can imagine. It will be surreal having you back driving me nuts in a body again. I can't wait to pinch you and make you squeal." I smiled as Ellie stuck her tongue out and drifted off to go watch the last of the tourists heading to their vehicles. She couldn't eat, so watching us dine on steaks and all the fixings must drive her bonkers at times.

"Johnny! Stop that!"

Our werewolf had been itching behind his ear and I expected his leg to start thumping any minutes now.

"Ew. Do you have fleas or something?" Nathara wandered over at that moment and slapped at his hand to force him to stop. Then she ruffled his hair and sat down beside him.

"No fleas. A new shampoo that is not agreeing with me. You look delicious enough to nibble on. I've not seen you in so short an outfit in quite some time, my lovely."

Indeed, Nathara was in tiny shorts and a too-tight top that showed off her magnificent body. Long black hair, lilac eyes, and pale, pearlescent skin had most every male she wandered past thinking naughty thoughts and trying not to get caught looking by their significant others. It was a losing battle—Nathara was stunning. Especially in the goth, witchy, porcelain doll way she usually dressed. Not this evening. If I had to guess, I would think Pandora had gotten under her skin and this was a small way she could assert her feminine wiles and not be overt about it like Bella, Serena, and Sydney—only in their case, I think it had more to do with Dorie being a crossroads demon.

Dara gave Nathara the once over and sniffed. Oh, brother!

"If you dress like a tramp to attract attention, you wind up with fleas!"

This disembodied voice came floating out of a large tote bag that Dara carried everywhere with her. Daracha Bristol was from solid Welsh stock. She loved giving tourists and those in the Breed world readings by scrying her crystal ball for the answers from the Great Beyond. That was who uttered that mishmash of phrases just now. Madame Myna was glowing and swirling around her round orb like an agitated peacock—she resided in the crystal ball and was Dara's sidekick—just don't tell Madame that!

"No good will come to those who sell their wares while ruffling hair."

"Tell your glowing ball to shut it before I bring her to

the auction house." Nathara was all talk and would never harm Madame Myna, but her surly attitude probably had something to do with being called out on her small display of attention-seeking—and losing her aloof ennui enough to let us see how much Pandora got to her after all.

"Oh! Is that your potato salad, Dara? You make the best." Nathara certainly knew how to deflect the attention off herself and focus it on a now-blushing Dara who'd nodded. Indeed, no one could make homemade potato salad like our druid. I don't know if she added a bit of magic to her concoction, but one bite of it ruined you for anyone else's.

I watched with hooded eyes and Nathara leaned into Johnny, stretching her arms up and hooking them around his neck while placing her feet on Tor's lap. He obliged her pouty brow wiggle by beginning to massage her exceedingly pretty and bare feet.

Grr.

"Did we tap that keg yet?" I grumbled.

"On it." Serena wandered over to the big barrel carrying two empty pitchers and while Sydney helped, she opened the tap so the golden liquid could flow. Filling the two pitchers quickly, she placed one on our table and the other by Dara.

"So, Maggie. I noticed you have your hands full with men throwing themselves at you again. Wasn't that Danny Grayson, your former lover I spied kissing you by your tent? And who is the mysterious tall dark and bespeckled man who keeps following you around like Pepe le Pew?" Nathara knew she struck a chord when I flattened my lips and snuck a peek at how Tor would react to her taunting.

"Do not call that idiot that. Daniel was never a lover. A fumbling hormone maybe—but never a lover!" I protested, taking a sip of my beer.

"Then why did you let him get all chummy? I mean, I would never seduce a man unless I fully intended on going the distance—if you know what I mean." Nathara shifted a little and one foot hitched up to Tor's shoulder where she allowed her toes to lightly trail down Tor's arm until her foot settled back in his capable hands so the massage could continue.

Grr. Again!

"I think he followed us here," said Bella, who'd just sailed by on her roller skates. She had a bit of foam on her upper lip which means she'd already had a pint or two!

"You think?" I sighed inwardly. Could we not change the subject to something less me?

Antoine came over with a tray of juicy steaks and all talk stopped while we became the carnivores we were...all except Dara who ate her salads and some kind of vegan-lentil mixture that smelled like the earth.

Spinning to a stop to grab a plate and a juicy steak of her own, Bella nodded in the direction of the opposite side of the fairgrounds that we could just make out through our RVs. "Take a look at lover boy number one! Where do you think he got a pumpkin that big this early in the season? It's June! You don't usually see jack-o-lanterns that massive until October!"

Lover boy?

I tracked to where Bella had pointed in time to see Levi Patel carrying what had to be a one-hundred-and-fifty pound pumpkin on one shoulder while maneuvering around the stalls of the various vendors who were closing up shop for the evening. The way he held it had me realize it was probably made out of some kind of light material and wasn't real, and I said so.

"That isn't real. And look! It has a massive hole on the bottom like someone could easily use as a headdress—a pumpkin head! Well, at least he's heading in the right direction with it—and stop calling him lover boy!" I spat.

Everyone laughed, although kindly—well, all except Tor who didn't even crack a smile, and Nathara, whose chuckle was laced with purest of evil.

The witch.

CHAPTER 6

T he next day was a half-day seeing as it was Sunday, and the fairgrounds didn't open until noon. We'd close early as well, which meant another gathering of friends and relatives. This left me and Ellie dragging Bob back to Lily's home where she'd offered to make breakfast for us. I was on my second cup of coffee, watching as she began flipping pancakes in earnest.

"Where's Dorie? I hoped we could continue our conversation from yesterday," said Ellie. I was correct in my assumption the two had gotten along famously and it was evident Ellie was upset the crossroads demon wasn't among us.

"She's around somewhere. I just hope she hasn't decided to go torture your friends. She grumbled some-thing about Bella being too big for her britches that's giving me nightmares!" Lily said with a frown.

"I don't understand why those three are being so belligerent! Dorie is a free spirit. Fun, lively, likes to laugh, loves a good party—it's like she and I are kindred spirits!" lamented Ellie.

I knew my sister missed hanging out with friends and running wild doing all manner of things that gave my father white hair, but to say she and a crossroads demon were kindred spirits might be going a bit far.

"Why the animosity? Did Pandora say?" I asked Lily.

"Oh, something about elementals and demons being at war for eternity it seems, and only until recently, which for them could be twenty years or two thousand, did certain factions call a truce. I don't think Pandora's kind abide by any rules, so elementals and other demons mistrust them and go on the attack whenever they cross paths."

Lovely.

"How are you holding up with that Daniel Grayson guy showing up?" asked Andrea. Lily's cousin was the youngest in our foursome, and she seemed to thrive on romance and drama.

"Please don't remind me. He insisted he didn't follow me and that it was all a misunderstanding. I could wring your neck for putting those thoughts in his head, Ellie." I went on to explain in detail the sordid tale to Lily, who listened on with sympathy. Then she regaled us about her college days and a boy who'd inadvertently decided he was gay after she gave her virginity to him. By the time we were done swapping old war stories, tears were pouring out of our eyes and our sides ached from laughing so hard.

This was nice. This is exactly what I hoped my week would be like. Perhaps the drama would move on in the form of one Daniel Grayson wrapping up his sudden need to go antiquing, and Levi Patel would sell out his wares and move on to his next destination—or go crawl under a rock where he belonged. My thoughts turned to Tor, and I scowled. This did not go unnoticed by Andrea.

"Uh, oh. You look like Lily did when she was having problems with Lorcan," Andrea giggled.

"I'm still having problems with Lorcan—he of the "I must go aid the evil Tiffany Clarkson, of the Sweet Briar Clarkson's and her stupid rabbit, Lucifer," complained Lily.

"She named her rabbit Lucifer?" I asked.

"Yeah. And she's a deputy so we have something in common. You with that idiot detective and me with Lorcan's ex fake girlfriend!"

"Fake?" I looked at Lily to further explain and she informed us that Tiffany hadn't ever truly dated Lorcan Reid. She was a way to get back at our cousin Nora who broke up with him and took him back more times than was remotely decent. Lorcan was too nice an empath and didn't see Nora was playing him like a fiddle. A nastier cousin we could not have. Nora was Cousin Iona's daughter and is currently estranged from the family. She even spoke badly about her mother's sister, Adelaide. Things were tense where Nora was concerned, and I didn't envy Lily for having to live in the same town as the nasty witch.

"You have to point Tiffany out to me if you get the chance."

"Oh, I'm sure she'll be around. She lives to torture me!" said Lily. "So, spill, why the glum face?"

I told them about how Tor and I had kissed once on a case and the electricity between us was incredible. But then I went on to describe our recent issues, the most glaringly obvious one being Danny Grayson—although Levi Patel coming on to me didn't help matters any.

"Oh, he needs to get over himself! What is it with men anyway? It's perfectly fine for them to play hero for ex-girl-friends, but the minute we have an old flame show up they go caveman on us," cried Lily.

"Uh, Lily? I think you are projecting here," Andrea chided.

"Oh...yeah. Sorry!" She gave me a sheepish look, but she wasn't wrong in her observations.

"Tor will need to work this out on his own. I won't play games and he will either respect me and know my character or will sulk into the arms of another." Thoughts of Nathara and her wandering feet made me want to throw something. I refrained from doing so and tossed a bit of pancake to Lily's cat instead. Wicked sniffed it, gave me a dismissive glare, but gobbled it up anyway.

Bob appeared despondent in his prison crate, so I got up and slipped him a piece as well.

Lily grinned at the interaction, and I admired the way my beautiful cousin looked when there was a smile on her face instead of a frown.

My beautiful raven-haired cousin had changed a bit since the last time we were here. More confident and less worried about every magical thing to cross her path, this new Lily Sweet had something more, especially when one looked deeply into her eyes. She had peace. I guess rescuing both of her parents and reuniting her family could do that to one's outlook. Yet I still detected worry, and I assumed her thoughts were with Charlie and Adelaide as they sought the answers to heal the scars Charlie was dealing with.

I noticed Ellie staring at Lily as well, and it dawned on me that Lorcan might be a sore subject for my sister. They'd kissed once under the bleachers of the old high school, and Lorcan all but admitted he was trying to erase Lily's memory from his mind with someone who looked an awful lot like her. Even though Ellie and I were fraternal twins, she had the black hair from our mother's side, while I got the flaming red from the Croys. Sitting all together in one room, you could certainly pick out the similarities between us. Lily belatedly remembered about that kiss and blushed—quickly assessing if her words had upset Ellie.

"I'm fine. It was teenaged angst and the heat of the moment. We were messing around is all. And you, my dear, are a lucky woman because man oh man can Lorcan kiss!"

We laughed and resumed our meal.

"These pancakes are to die for!" I proclaimed.

"Quick, grab a few and feed them to Danny and Levi Patel," giggled Ellie.

If she only knew how prophetic those words would become.

THE MORNING WENT by too quickly and I found myself lugging Bob back to my RV, changing quickly, then heading out to start my workday. I made sure to give Bob extra snuggles since he was so despondent over the rebukes his cousin Wicked gave him all morning. Cats. You never knew why some got along and others became mortal enemies. I gave Bob an extra treat and told him to buck up.

"You never know, buddy. Maybe Wicked will come around before we leave, and you will become fast friends."

Not likely.

Pandora had shown up and Ellie decided to spend the day with her new BFF. I detected a bit of jealousy on Lily's part and wondered if she'd finally decided she enjoyed having her tagalong demon, and no longer wanted to share her with the rest of the world. She'd whispered to me when Ellie was chatting with Andrea that Dorie's sole purpose in life lately was trying to convince her they were destined to become the best of friends. Well, we'd be gone soon, and Lily could work on their issues...such as they were.

I knew Bella would be cranky today—she drank more beer than anyone last night and was still passed out in Dara's and her Winnebago. Dara was up early and doing the wash...I could see the sheets and unmentionables hanging on the clothesline she'd strung up from the corner of her RV to Antoine's. She waved as I passed, and I returned it with a smile pointing toward the tents with my coffee carafe.

It was cooler this morning. The humidity broke overnight, and I enjoyed the respite from the oppressive stickiness that we'd had for the last few days. I knew this interlude of cool air wouldn't last—summer in the south was never without muggy temperatures—but I'd take it when it came unexpectedly any day! The bird song brought me a sense of peace and I felt harmonious with my surroundings.

I took a bite out of a juicy peach Lily had gifted me from Jaemor Farms, a wonderful family farm that had the best produce in the state, a neat corn maze in the fall, and fried apple pies to die for, and I reveled in the flavor as the liquid went down my face and neck and into my shirt— and I didn't mind a bit. I planned on heading down for a bushel or two and would treat my crew to some cobbler and fresh-eating deliciousness.

As I approached my tent, I noticed the flap was open and moving back and forth in the breeze. Maybe Bella did come in without my knowing, and she was even now enjoying the cool wind that curled throughout our workspace.

As I entered the tent, two things struck me. One, it took a moment for the brightness of the afternoon to fade enough so I could make out the shadows and filtered light as my eyes became used to being indoors once more. And two, there was a man sitting on the ground, legs sprawled out in front of him, and he had a giant pumpkin firmly wedged on his head. He held something in his hand that looked like a small note, but it was obscured by the rose he was clutching.

Then I noticed a third thing. There seemed to be a dark puddle on the ground around him, and upon further inspection, I realized the liquid was blood.

I think I found Levi Patel—and he was almost certainly dead.

So much for peace and harmony!

CHAPTER 7

"Did you touch anything?"

Brian Chase, detective par excellence stood closer to me than I thought normal, but I wasn't going to back up to show how much he intimidated me just now.

"No. Not only did I not touch anything, I walked backward trying not to make more tracks than I already did."

Brian seemed satisfied with my answer but added one more which caused me to shudder.

"You didn't kill him, right, Maggie? I have to ask you this so please understand it's my job and is not personal."

"I didn't kill him. I didn't know him. And even if I did, I don't go around killing pesky men. I'm sure you are aware of how he's been acting around me and what transpired yesterday?"

Brian relaxed and stepped out of my personal space. Then it dawned on me what he'd been doing. "You're a Veritum, aren't you?"

He nodded yes and escorted me to the other side of a temporary tent the police had set up to interview people.

They had gone through my entire crew first, and Brian didn't seem surprised to hear about our extracurricular activities as paranormal monster-hunters.

Antoine strikes again.

I'm sure our esteemed vampire made sure to flash his badge and put in a call to The Order to clear things with the local police. Even now, Lily's nemesis, the annoyingly efficient Tiffany Clarkson of the Sweet Briar Clarkson's was interviewing the distraught Dev Patel. The poor man seemed beyond confused as to why his cousin was in my tent in the first place and had a pumpkin wedged firmly on his head.

After the police took all the photos they needed, I witnessed the gruesome removal of the pumpkin—which indeed was made out of a lightweight material—and grimaced at the look of death on the poor former appraiser.

I guess he wouldn't be pestering me for dates anymore.

I felt guilty even though the rational side of me knew I had nothing to do with any of this.

Still, my pesky admirer, my tent. I slapped him yesterday and threatened disembowelment and more in front of a vast audience of tourists and locals. Was it any wonder I was now getting surreptitious glances from the vast majority of looky-loos that had gathered to see what the fuss was about?

I wondered if it was too late to go crawl into bed with Bella and sleep the rest of the day away.

I could see a concerned-looking Danny Grayson hovering on the edge of the police barricade. His jurisdiction was so far from here, not even professional courtesy would work allowing him entry on an active investigation. So he just stewed and eyed me from afar.

Wait a minute! Someone had done this to Levi. Danny

was there when things heated up between the two and he had to be restrained when Levi kissed me. Could it be so easy?

"Brian. Wait up."

Rushing over to the police detective, I couldn't help but notice how the afternoon sky paled in comparison to the vibrant blue eyes that met mine—a question in them as he turned to hear what I had to say.

"You may want to have one of your people grab that man over there. He's a detective back in Mystic Valley, North Carolina where I live—well, where my dad has his compound we all congregate on when not touring. Anyway, Ellie may have spelled him making him think we are destined to be together." Brian blinked in surprise, and I hurriedly explained the reason behind the magic that we'd done on a human police officer.

"So, you see, he might not be in his right mind—the magical suggestion takes a long time to wear off—and he was already agitated with Levi Patel for coming on to me so strongly. Perhaps he deserves some scrutiny?"

"This is not good, Maggie. If Ellie spelled a human and he committed murder while under her influence? This could get ugly in a hurry—not just with our local Council, but The Order of Origin will step in and send a Geister-jäger in to deal with her," he warned.

"A Geister-what?" I looked at Brian in alarm.

"A professional ghost hunter. Their job is to round up ghosts who refuse to move on for one reason or another, and if they can't convince them to be recorded with The Order and move on, a demon collector swoops in and claims their soul. Ellie could be in big trouble. We need help." Brian shook his head at the mess we'd gotten ourselves into and I began to panic—on the inside, but still!

"Who can we turn to for help? I'm already a part of The Order! My dad?" I asked, wondering what Brian had up his sleeve.

"No, someone far more powerful and with more connections than anyone I know," he said, glancing around to see if anyone was listening. When Brian was satisfied no one would overhear what he had to say next, he leaned forward and whispered. "We need Adriana Dolce."

Oh, this was going to get interesting but quick.

"So we've been closed down? How is this fair? The main group is still selling and appraising, why have we been singled out?" Nathara was in a foul mood, and I knew she was itching to put the blame squarely on yours truly, despite our recent understanding where I'd helped keep her family secrets. She was prickly that way.

"Because Levi Patel wound up dead in Maggie's tent and she's the prime suspect," said Bella, then gave me an apologetic glance, "I mean, the general populace thinks she offed the poor man. The police have cleared her because that hunky Brian Chase sucked face with her and now he thinks she's innocent." Bella giggled, and I threw my napkin at her.

We were sitting on Lily's sunporch waiting for a spaghetti and meatball dinner complete with salad, rolls, and wine. Hopefully, plenty of wine.

"He did not suck my face! Brian is a Veritum. He used his talent to verify I was telling the truth. It's not like humans can employ this tactic! Sweet Briar is lucky to have him on hand to weed out the innocent from the real murderer," I sniffed. "The thing is, everyone else thinks I'm guilty and what point is having my tent open for business when I would have no customers in sight?"

"That's not why he shut us down," said Antoine quietly. "We need to be in on the investigation and we can't do that while worrying about appraising the mundane. It's not as if a long line of paranormals have been knocking at our door. Sweet Briar is a magnet for tourists—human ones. So, this won't hurt our bottom line. Estelle is reporting brisk business in any case."

My dad would be pleased—that is if his ghostly daughter doesn't wind up sucked into a battle between a ghost-hunter and a demon soul-taker that is.

"Who is this woman coming to speak with Ellie anyway? Lily said she knows their aunts?" Dara was worried about the meeting that Adriana Dolce had set up between Ellie and a ghost-hunter who came highly recommended by two witches who ran a tea and potion shop here in town.

"The Winters sisters said their niece, Samantha Geist, is the best in the business. My great-grandmother set it up so Samantha could meet with Ellie in a pretrial capacity—not that I think Ellie will wind up in trouble with our Council or The Origin." Lily added quickly.

"What will happen if they decide Ellie is at fault and they really do come for her?" Andrea asked worriedly, and I noticed she began scratching at her elbows. Lily pointed at her, and she stopped shamefacedly, so I deduced this was a longtime habit she was trying to overcome.

"Samantha told Adriana she has some favors she can call in and keep Ellie out of trouble—I hope anyway. This is all new to me," said Lily. "I didn't even know there was such a thing as ghost-hunters and demon soul-takers until this morning!"

"Don't you worry about a thing," Adriana waltzed in

the room just then taking us all in with a stern look. "Samantha is supposed to be second to none with this ghost-hunting stuff—and is a phenomenal paranormal detective. She certainly can help Brian figure out a thing or two about this case. And she has a long list of influential and important people she has helped, so methinks she can put out any and all fires."

Ellie looked hopeful at Adriana's statement, and I gave her a thumbs up which she returned, albeit halfheartedly.

"That name though! I hope she isn't like another Samantha we've had to deal with as of late!" Andrea began worrying her elbows again and I had to stifle the urge to snap my fingers in her direction.

"Oh?" I said instead, hoping someone would enlighten me.

"One of the people aiding the evil witch who destroyed my family separating us all twenty-odd years go is named Samantha. She is currently cooling her heels in the witch prison. But her niece, Rowan, has escaped to parts unknown. So, the name is kind of taboo around here," Lily said.

"Well, this Samantha will be nothing like Samantha Fairburn, may she rot in prison," grumbled Andrea.

Just then the doorbell rang, and I knew we'd be catching our first glimpse at a real-live geisterjäger! I just prayed she was as good as everyone was saying—or Ellie was in deep ectoplasmic doo-doo!

CHAPTER 8

The woman who sat across from me enjoying Lily's spaghetti and meatball dinner was unlike any woman I'd ever seen before. Her eyes were the color of storms, and her hair was a steely silver-grey that hung in cascading waves around her shoulders. She was tall. Like *really* tall—Serena and Sydney immediately looked to see if she had worn heels. She hadn't.

Despite the silver hair, Samantha Geist looked young. Almost as young as Bella, but not quite. If I had to place an age to match her face, I'd say twenty-two or three. In actuality, I believed the woman was in her early to late forties. A babe in our world, still, but hardly a baby. She didn't speak much, hadn't cracked a smile despite the jovial mood most of the guests were in, and had an air of sorrow about her that I found haunting—yet compelling.

Samantha had a smattering of light freckles and wore no makeup, yet she was stunning. Of that, there was no doubt. One only had to watch the men cast veiled looks in her direction to see how she was affecting the opposite sex. Yet this didn't faze her in the slightest. If anything, it made her more pensive and introverted. Or perhaps she was distracted with the discourse those gathered had been bantering about.

"I still say Brian needs to pin this on that Daniel Grayson. Cop or no cop. Who follows a woman from one state to another under the guise of antique shopping? I know he's spelled, but come on!" Johnny was five glasses deep in a rosé wine that packed quite the punch—at least as far as werewolves went.

"Perhaps we need to interrogate him ourselves? Leave this Brian Chase out of it altogether. No?" Sven, our resident shifter was warily peering at Samantha as he made that bold statement, but I knew he wasn't a fan of bringing her on board in this latest investigation we'd been drawn into through no fault of our own. Well, OK, Ellie spelled Danny, and if he was guilty, we had to take some responsibility for it. Guilty by association and all that. But Sven, a one-time assassin, had his own way of dealing with issues that cropped up from time to time—and Levi Patel's murder definitely fell into that category.

"Why the pumpkin though?" Dara was fixated on the manner of Levi's death. "Why go to the trouble of sticking that ridiculous thing on his head? Wouldn't you want to rush out of there as soon as possible after committing murder? And how was the poor man done in anyway?"

"Blood and gore, skin and bone. A knife to the neck sent Levi home." Madame Myna intoned from her spot on the shelf to my right.

"That was no knife," I uttered darkly. "Someone stuck a chopstick in his neck, then stabbed him in the heart with the other for good measure. The poor man looked like a voodoo doll with pins stuck in it!" I informed the horrified group.

"Knife, chopstick. They're all the same!" Madame

Myna sniffed then her crystal ball went dark. I think I insulted her.

Dabbing at her lips then replacing her napkin on her lap, one couldn't help but notice how graceful Samantha moved. Everything she did reminded me of a swan, gilding across a pond—or a ballerina pretending to be one.

"Has a paranormal medical examiner been called in to examine the body? And did they give the time of death?" she asked softly.

"Yes. Brian called Doc Clarkston, who took over recently and he called it at around 8 AM. Actually, he said a good estimate put it fifteen minutes before and after that time. So anywhere from 7:45 to 8:15 should be about right." This from Jake, who I'd just found out was an attorney. Even though I've known him for years—his mother is the sister of Cousin Iona's husband, Owen, making us related by marriage—it somehow slipped past me that he had gone into that profession. Keeping up with friends and relatives when on the road most of the year is proving difficult.

Perhaps Ellie needed his business card.

I eyed Samantha and was startled to see she'd been contemplating me while I was lost to my musings.

"Why do you think this man became infatuated with you? Had you ever met him before?" she asked me.

"Um, no. I mean, Ellie noticed he was following us closely on our way down from North Carolina. He's been in Asheville getting new items to auction, but he was a fellow appraiser like we are. Only I'd never run across him before. He has ties to this town because his cousin, Dev, lives here."

Samantha nodded after a moment then cut her eyes to Ellie.

"You were the first to notice he was following your RV?"

Ellie just nodded yes—she couldn't bring herself to speak.

"Curious."

"We have to figure out who would have a motive to kill this man. I mean, it seems obvious to me it's Daniel Grayson. He thinks Maggie is pining for him and has been spelled to be interested in her, when in reality he dumped her years ago!" Bella stated, trying to be helpful.

Hey!

He didn't actually dump me per se... we just..." Everyone turned sympathetic eyes my way and I realized my sordid tale of thinking I'd been impregnated by the man—a boy at the time—had made the rounds, and my shame was complete. "OK, fine. He dumped me. He's a total jerk!" I threw my hands up in the air and sat back in a huff.

"Do you often get this heated when upset?" Samantha asked, and I began to chafe.

My temper was rising, and I found this woman to be too calm and way too collected for my liking. Before I could reply, however, there came a banging sound from the kitchen and Pandora walked in.

"Hey! I'm gone for half a day and y'all throw a party and leave me out? Whoa! And look what we have here! Hiya, Spooky! Long time no see! Who called you up from the nether? Any demons catch you slacking on the job lately? Or are you still mooning over any lucifant you come across? Well, a certain lucifant, anyway."

Spooky? Lucifant?

Was I the only one here confused by Doric's words?

"How was I supposed to know Pandora and Samantha crossed paths before—and are on opposite teams? I thought a ghost-hunter simply convinced a lost soul to move on. How was I supped to know they are mortal—or immortal in this case—enemies with demons called lucifants?" Adriana groused while sipping her espresso.

"Dorie needs to stop playing with fire—literally. Who knew she and Samantha go way back? How old is Samantha anyway?" Lily asked.

"Around two hundred give or take."

"What?" I was dumbfounded. "She's a witch, no? How can that be?"

"Samantha's mother was a witch; her father is a revenant. Hermione and Hortense are related on her mother's side," Adriana informed us.

"Wait. Stop. Explain, please? What's a revenant?" asked Lily, making it obvious yet again that she hadn't been raised among the paranormal.

"They are undead. Not unlike a vampire, yet more ghost than bloodsucker. Hey! Wait a minute. Do you think?" I looked at Ellie whose eyes had grown the size of saucers. "Do you think that is what happened to Ellie? Is she part revenant now?"

Samantha came walking back into the den from Lily's side porch where she'd been on the phone consulting with someone on her team. "Of course, Ellie is a revenant. Not by birth, but by magic. Once you reverse the curse placed upon her, she will continue to be a revenant. She will retain her body, but Ellie will always be able to walk in shadow. She has become a shade, yet still a witch. If you like, I could train you to do what I do for a living." This, Samantha addressed to my shell-shocked sibling who looked like she was about to burst into tears.

"Am I cursed with this? I don't want to be a revenant!" Ellie wailed.

Samantha considered my sibling for a long minute then shrugged. Taking the seat across from me, she placed her phone on the side table then folded her hands on her lap. "You have no choice. Once you've been turned, there is no "cure" since you have basically been injected with revenant blood—kind of the way once demon blood is in you, it becomes part of you." She addressed this last part to Lily, making me wonder if there was something there of which we had not been aware. Lily had demon blood?

"I wonder what a revenant mixed with a lucifant would produce?" Pandora snickered, giving Samantha a side glance then began contemplating her nails.

For the first time since she'd arrive, I noticed Samantha having an emotion other than quiet and reserved. Her eyes flashed in Pandora's direction, and she clenched her hands into fists. Ah, so the icy demeanor could be heated up! I wondered at the relationship these two women had over the years, but I didn't think it my place to ask.

"How do you two know each other?" asked Ellie.

Apparently, minding her own business was alien to my sister. I nervously coughed giving a slight shake to my head, but Ellie either didn't see or chose to ignore it. Instead, she poked the geisterjäger who seemed more upset by the query than Dorie did. "I mean, it's obvious you know each other," she stated.

"I don't know why that is any of your concern."

"Oh, don't be such a wet fish, Spooky. The girl can't help being curious."

"Blanket."

"What?" Dorie blinked in confusion.

Samantha responded through gritted teeth. "Blanket. It's 'don't be such a wet blanket,' not fish."

"Well, that doesn't make any sense. Who ever heard of a wet blanket? I mean, sure...if you just washed it. But fish are in water and that means they are wet. Wet blanket? Not so much."

I could see the strain of not responding to Pandora was making Samantha lose some of her stoicism and appear more human—er—witchlike. I still couldn't wrap my head around the fact that she could turn into a ghost at whim, but it would explain why revenants made such stellar lost soul finders. The animosity between the two women must have something to do with the fact that if Samantha failed to convince a soul to move on or worse—said soul turned violent, effectively becoming a poltergeist—a demon, and lucifants would swoop in and steal that soul to their realm. Something must have happened in their past to have Dorie acting so snarky.

Turning once more to address Ellie, Samantha cleared her throat, all business once more. "I have spoken to my contacts at The Order. While they were mildly concerned no one from your family reported the fact that you returned as a ghost and that you do not seem to have the ability to move on—at least I assume this, has no light ever beckoned or an urge to move on overcome you? No? Then we will move on my advice that you are not held accountable for this unfortunate occurrence, but the attempt to reunite you with your body must take place at once."

Samantha saw concern cross Ellie's face and softened her words with a slight smile, then continued. "It's not as scary as it sounds. I will take samples from you, almost like giving blood, only in your case I extract a bit of your essence and send it in for testing. Once we have a better understanding of how you were turned and what dark magic was added to keep you in a permanent ghostly state, we can begin to reverse it. I will need the help of your cousin Lily and Adriana here, since it will take three dark witches to work the spell and bring you back to the living."

Lily's eyes grew wide at this announcement, but Adriana continued to look shrewdly at our visitor. "But what about this situation we have? Will you remain to help Brian with the case?" she asked.

"I'm going to override his authority and take over the case since I'm here. I've opened a file on Levi Patel and will hunt for his soul. He may have already moved on. But if not, I will find him and try to make sense of his last moments."

"Make sense? I don't understand," said Lily.

Samantha turned her enigmatic eyes on my cousin and asked her a question instead of responding to her query. "You have a ghost living here on and off, don't you? And if I'm not mistaken, the spirit of Moira Fortune-Croy has been known to appear to you from time to time. Is there any reason why you've not reported these lost souls to the authorities?"

Lily appeared shocked at first, then guilty, but that lasted all of two seconds before she began to frown in a way that made me think of Adriana.

"Don't you threaten my ghosts! I'm sure Moira and Edith have good reasons why they haven't moved on yet. Don't think you can come here and start pushing everyone around and take my friend and great aunt's spirit just because of some rules..."

"You'd risk a lucifant to come and take them then?"

"I... huh." Lily went from furious outrage to confused and cut her eyes to Adriana for some backup.

"Samantha, lighten up. Moira had something similar happen to her by her own hand. I think she is running around here as a revenant or something similar. We don't have time for that right now. When Ellie's case progresses, we can address Moira then—and only then. I will deal with any and all lucifants if they decide to show up unannounced." Adriana remained friendly but there was a steel-like reprimand behind her words.

"As for Edith, she is a very helpful ally and will move on in due time. She is hardly lost. Edith has all her faculties and isn't showing any symptoms of having turned adrift and flummoxed. Now, if I may suggest? Work with Brian. He's a veritum. Don't count on finding Levi Patel as the only course of action. The Council is squawking and wants someone on the case other than one of us which is why I sought your aid. You may have people that owed you a favor my dear, but don't forget, you owe me one—and I'm calling it in." Samantha actually blushed at these words, much to my astonishment, then nodded once. "Good. While you are busy keeping the authorities happy and not looking too closely at Ellie's predicament, my great-grand-daughter and her friends here will get to the bottom of this mess. With all of you working on it, we should have our baddie caught in no time! The key thing is to keep the authorities from trapping Ellie and doing all manner of tests on her. Capisce?"

Lily reached her hand out to Ellie who'd gasped, and we locked eyes. No one would take my sister away from me and live to talk about it—authorities or not. We had work to do and little time to waste.

CHAPTER 9

"**T**hat woman is creepy," Andrea said, sipping her coffee later that evening while we gathered around Lily's kitchen table.

We cleared the house of everyone except me, Ellie, Lily, Lorcan, Jake, Andrea, and Bella. Oh...and Pandora. I thought the demon had skedaddled after Samantha, but she remained behind to see what plans we'd come up with, adding her two cents here and there until I thought Bella would blow.

The rest of my team went back to our site to get some sleep since Brian pulled some strings and they would now be allowed to continue with the appraisals since only my tent was a crime scene. It would remain closed for business —leaving Bella and me free to help solve the case. Before Antoine left, he offered the team as backup.

"Just keep me updated and say the word—we will be here if you need us, Mags."

Dara wanted to stay behind with Madame Myna and give us a hand with the case, but Antoine ushered her out, with her complaining all the way back to the fairgrounds, I was certain of it.

It didn't get past me that Tor chose to go with the rest of my group and not offer to stay. I was now too angry with him and his insecurities to give a flippity-flip, and if he thought I was going to apologize for something I had no control over, he had another think coming.

Brian Chase showed up, and I was struck again at just how incredibly handsome the man was. Longish black hair, eyes the color of the Pacific during a tempest, and a killer smile—I wondered at how the man remained single all these years, then remembered Lily and he were an item for a time. I turned to gaze at Lorcan, then smiled. Lily went for the solid and reliable—and the also incredibly good-looking empath chose to not get caught up in the intensity that was one Brian Chase, detective and veritum. But I could tell the man still held a candle for my cousin—so could Lorcan for that matter.

She placed a coffee at Brian's spot and pushed a tray of cookies toward him. Brian gratefully took a few and munched while he spoke. He looked like he hasn't eaten much since this mess happened.

"If you thought she was creepy, you should've seen the guy that showed up from The Order of Origin. That man looked like an ancient werewolf who lost himself to the beast within. I thought he would transform and gobble up everyone in sight for a moment there. Talk about intense." Brian placed a file on the table then sighed before he continued. "I don't know why I'm sharing this with you all, but...well, it is what it is. I know you are going to try and solve this case on your own, so I am going to give you details that no one else is privy to. Just don't let them get out, OK?"

We all nodded, and he began to read from the notes in the file.

"One, Levi Patel was killed with those chopsticks. No magic was used that we could find."

Everyone erupted with questions causing Brian to hold his hands up to settle our group.

"Let me get everything out and then we can brainstorm. No magic. It kind of backs up Maggie's theory that it might be this Daniel Grayson fella. I would hate for it to be a cop, but no one is above the law...so if he did this, we will get him. Two, a cryptic note was left behind so that leads me to ask if you've ever received anything like this prior to this incident?"

Picking up an oddly put-together note protected by a plastic baggy, Brian passed it around the room until it landed in front of me.

Those who misbehave need to pay the price. Maggie, you belong to me. I didn't have to think twice about removing someone who would treat you as his own. I am watching out for you. I am watching. Always.

"Oh, sick. That's a sicko mind. That has Danny written all over it," Ellie whined. "Remember how he used to tell you what to wear and who to hang around with when you were dating in high school? It sounds just like him! Brian, go arrest him now!"

"I've never received anything like this before. I mean...could this be because of what Ellie put in Danny's mind? If he killed this Levi Patel because of it, I'm worried no manner of favors and help Samantha is holding over some people will matter. They are going to come for my sister!" I cried and ran my hands through my hair until it began taking on a life of its own.

"There's more," Brian began. "We found photographs of Maggie on Levi's phone. He had some developed at the pharmacy and they were on the front seat of his SUV. I think he was going to do something with them...because who makes photos today when you can store them digitally? But it also looks like someone else—probably the killer—found them as well, because that vehicle looks like someone took all their rage out on it. Your photos were shredded, the car's windows were bashed in, and the seats were slashed. It's like a madman went off on it, and that's the thing—whoever this guy is, he's totally mental. You need to be extra careful Maggie."

"Is that everything?" I managed to croak out.

"No. I thought you should know Daniel Grayson disappeared. Right after we questioned him initially, he agreed to come down to the station to fill out his statement and profess his innocence. Only he never came in. We have an APB out on him as a person of interest and put a magical web around the town. If he tries to leave or enter, or if he's already out of the town's limits, it should alert. I say should, because we didn't have enough of his personal items on hand to create a stronger spell. All I had was a pen he touched so the spell is rather weak. But at least it's something." Brian finished his update and stood to leave. "Just don't stay alone for the time being, and we will do everything we can to find this guy and bring him in."

We bade Brian a good night then sat staring at nothing for quite some time, lost in our own thoughts.

"That man has the most incredible hair. He needs to let it grow even longer," sighed Pandora, "I have to control myself from running my hands through it every time he's near—or this one here will snap her fingers at me."

Lily scowled at Pandora.

"Did you not just do the nasty with Steve in this very house on this very table?" I sat up and pushed away from the offending piece of furniture since I just had my head resting on it.

"Oh, pooh! That was weeks ago now."

"Two weeks. And that's not the point. The point is you are involved with Steve—not that I know how someone like you is going to have any kind of longevity with a fairly young male witch!"

"Someone like me. You mean a crossroads demon? Or are you getting personal here?" Pandora looked affronted, and I wondered where Lily was going with this line of questioning—and why.

"I mean, are you planning on moving on to Brian next? Won't that hurt Steve's feelings?" Lily began to worry her bottom lip and reached out to stop Andrea from scratching her elbows.

"Lily. You can't be that naïve. Come on woman! Steve and I are not looking for anything long-term. This is a bit of fun and..."

"And I don't like it one bit. If he gets hurt..."

Pandora stood, and Bella began to growl again. This set Bob off who was still trapped in his crate with an irate Wicked sitting on top of it looking like the queen of all she surveyed. His meowing startled her into a hissing fit, and before I knew what had happened, Pandora slammed out of the house into the night leaving us looking at anything but Lily.

Lorcan put his arm around her and gave her shoulder a squeeze. "Lily, I don't think..."

"No. You don't, do you? So do me a favor and lay off the advice."

Uh-oh.

I had a feeling Lily was reacting from circumstances out of her control. That Tiffany Clarkson must be grating on her nerves to the extent she was projecting the ire she was feeling about that situation on anyone and everyone— and Pandora just got the brunt of the hurt and confusion Lily was experiencing.

I felt like an added burden and made to stand up and take my leave.

"No, Maggie, sit. Stay. I'm sorry. I'm just not thinking straight." Lily took in a deep breath then let it out slowly. I noticed she hadn't apologized to Lorcan for her outburst and I hoped the two of them could work out their issues.

"Dorie is right. Brian *does* have dreamy hair. He could even get away with a man bun," Lorcan stated.

Lily looked at him in horror.

Irritation forgotten for a moment, her focus was now on something that she must have very deep feelings about because her face had turned an ugly shade of red.

"No one can get away with a man bun except for Michael Hutchence!"

"Not him again!" Jake rolled his eyes and looked over at me. "Lily has a thing for '80s rock stars that I can barely remember."

"That's because you have poor taste in music," Lily snapped, turning a fierce glare in Jake's direction.

"Fine! Who today could pull off a man bun then?" Jake chided.

"I don't know. Brendan Urie?"

"They guy with the poufy lips? Are you kidding me?"

"Ooh! He's dreamy!" said Andrea, "I love Panic at the Disco." Ellie nodded in agreement.

My friends didn't bother to return to serious matters when Samantha Geist walked back in the room, stopping short when Lorcan lobbed a question at her. "What actor or musician today do you think could pull off a man bun?"

Samantha looked like a deer in the headlights, and I could see her trying to make sense of Lorcan's query. "Um, I don't...I guess that actor that plays Loki?"

"Tom Hiddleston? Really?" Lorcan and Jake recoiled and shared a look.

"I mean, he's, um..." Samantha looked like she wished she hadn't accepted Lily's invitation to stay with her and would have rather taken a room at the little motel we passed on the way into town.

"I like Tom Hiddleston. He could totally pull off a man bun." I gave Samantha a friendly grin, and she smiled back. My estimation of her went up a notch.

"Now I like Chris Hemsworth for a man bun. He's got the right look," said Lorcan, and I realized he started this discussion to distract Lily from the tangent she was on and let her know it was OK to be mad—but also reminding her that in the not-so-long-ago past it was *her* who was mooning over a man. One she was still friendly with and had just offered coffee and treats.

"Why? Just because they share a continent? What does Chris Hemsworth have to do with Michael's perfect hair?" Lily protested.

"And she's off," said Jake sighing once more.

"You stay out of it. You told me your man crush is Ryan Reynolds, and you're dead to me now!"

"What's wrong with Ryan Reynolds? I'm kind of crushing on the man a bit myself!" cried Lorcan.

"Ugh! That's it. I can't take this conversation another second. Now if you said Orlando Bloom, we'd have something," Lily grumbled. "You guys are so predictable. Ryan Reynolds! Please!"

"Oh, so that's how it is. He isn't even Australian. He's like from Iceland or Scotland or another *land* I can't recall," Lorcan groused then turned to the room for help.

"England."

"Come again?"

"Orlando Bloom is from England. Although his mother grew up in India and lived in Tasmania...so he has ties to Australia," I offered.

"Well, that doesn't mean anything! Lily is obviously fixated on one man—I will never be able to compete. I might as well shave my head bald."

"Don't you dare!" Lily stood, pointing her finger at Lorcan with such a look of horror on her face we all burst out laughing—except for Samantha. She began to scrutinize Lorcan as if visualizing him bald and liking what he'd look like with no hair.

After a few seconds, Lily's countenance went from agitated to self-deprecating and she too, began to laugh. "You may not have Michael's hair, but don't you ever let me hear you talk about shaving any of that off or you will live to regret it, buster!"

"As you wish!"

"And don't think I don't know what you just did there, either" sniffed Lily.

"Princess Bride?" I side-whispered to Jake.

"Princess Bride. It's a thing," he responded.

Nodding, I smiled to myself over the movie reference, then became somber once more. This momentary respite could not detract from the fact some sicko—probably one who I knew and had dated in my youth—was fixated on me and out there on the loose. That Danny had chosen to kill Levi Patel still shocked me to my core, and I couldn't help but feel guilty and burdened with the fact that had I'd handled things differently, we wouldn't be in this mess to begin with.

I left Danny to Ellie, and while her power of suggestion usually did the trick and got us out of countless messes, this time around it backfired—and how. She'd been so worried about having the police in Mystic Valley forget about what had happened at our compound, she didn't take the time to follow through on her thoughts to make Danny believe I still had a thing for him. Who knew he was such a loose cannon?

I certainly didn't see him as the psycho-stalking type!

"Hey, Maggie. I'm sorry. We sort of took over a minute here. We lost sight of what is most important. We need to figure out what our next steps should be. How do we find Daniel Grayson and what do we do when we catch up with him?" Lily asked.

"You're going to investigate?" Samantha asked curiously.

"We have to. Maggie and Ellie need our help. We stick together in this family and whether we are related by blood or are close friends, we don't leave something so important for others to take care of," said Andrea. "We take care of it ourselves!"

"What will you do?" Samantha didn't seem disturbed by this revelation, and I realized she was more on our side than I'd thought.

"I think we need to set a trap!" said Andrea. "I mean. He said he's watching her. Always. Well, I'm not sure if that is the boastful rantings of a lunatic, but since he's a human, it's not like the man can truly see Maggie 24/7. That means he's using traditional methods to spy on her— if he is. So, let's set a trap and nab the nutcase!"

"I like the way Andrea is thinking. This could be a

highly effective way of catching our mouse—by becoming the cat," I said.

"Only he's no mouse!" argued Lily. "What we have here is one dirty rat. Now let's go get him!"

"Meroo!" said Wicked.

Bob just hissed. *Again.*

CHAPTER 10

"Maggie! What are you doing out here in this hot June weather?" Garrison Black was walking by the makeshift table Antoine had set up for me in an area of the fairgrounds that locals could rent by the week to sell used junk. Occasionally an antique piece would show up that would be a great find for someone on the hunt, but for the most part, this section saw old toys and clothing, housewares, and other items gently—or even harshly—used.

He was dressed coolly in cotton shorts and a shirt, with a white Panama hat. Following close on his heels were Sandy and Cassie Booker, Estelle's capable, yet churlish twin assistants, who wore identical jean shorts and turquoise T-shirts with our Mystic Antiques and Uniques Caravan logo printed on them.

"I guess you've heard what happened? Yeah, well the show must go on, so they got me this spot so I can keep doing my job."

"Pity you have to work at all," said Garrison in reply.

"Yeah, because Maggie has it bad having to sit all day,"

argued Cassie. "Try doing what we do for Estelle. She's a dragon! I only get fifteen minutes to sit and eat something, then it's go, go, go all day! Wouldn't you rather be inside with the main outfit?"

Sandy nodded in agreement and added, "If we *get* fifteen minutes. How are your sales? Do you need anything? I still don't understand why you are way out here. Don't we have an extra tent?"

The two girls rapid-fired questions at me at a dizzying pace and I felt a headache coming on. I glanced at Garrison, and he shrugged in sympathy. I let the girls complain for another minute or so then cleared my throat.

"OK, ladies. I think you'd better hurry along. The dragon is approaching."

Cassie yelped and spied Estelle heading our way with a frown figuring prominently on her face.

"I'm out of here!" Sandy squawked.

"What were those two doing out here?" Estelle came up to my table, hands on her hips, watching as Cassie and Sandy scurried off toward the main building.

"Checking on me. Maybe letting off a little steam as well," I chuckled.

"Those girls whine like my Dale did whenever I'd drag him to the theater." Estelle smiled, but I could see her getting emotional at the memory. I reached my hand out and gave her arm a little squeeze. Dale was the one murdered last month by that deranged ancient strix vampire being that sent Bella on her one-upping challenge with Serena and Sydney. He was one of our trusted humans and my family felt the guilt of his demise greatly. My father took care of all the expenses for the funeral and upped Estelle's salary, but nothing he did would bring her husband back.

"What are you doing here, Garrison?"

"Checking on Maggie. But now I need to get back to work. I will stop by later with some water or something for you, Maggie, unless there is something else you need?"

"Thanks, but no. My cousin will be showing up with her friends later this evening and we may go grab a bite to eat out somewhere. But water would be nice."

Garrison tipped his hat and left, heading in the same direction as the twins.

Estelle waited until he was far away from us then sighed, grabbing the chair beside me and sat. "I never let them catch me resting. This way I can be a drill sergeant."

"I think they mentioned something about a dragon," I laughed.

Estelle chuckled then turned to me resting her chin in her hands. "What's going on with you and the hunky Scotsman? Am I detecting a note of trouble in the romance department?"

"Tor and I didn't have much of a chance on our first date with Daniel Grayson showing up." Estelle was a close friend, so the grapevine got around to informing her of my mishap. "But that's not it, Estelle. I shouldn't have to be made to feel guilty about something I had no control over, and I think Tor is acting ridiculous. He saw Danny kiss me and Levi fawning over me and turned into a petulant child about it. I don't need that kind of man." I said.

Estelle had been with us so long, she'd lived through my dating years with Danny and the entire, "oh no, I might be pregnant—nope, false alarm," fiasco that was the drama back when I was eighteen, so I didn't need to explain further. But it seemed my human friend knew some things I wasn't aware of regarding my paranormal world and set me straight with her next words.

"Oh, Mags, honey. You are so wrapped up in your world—which isn't so alien to me—that even *I* know about vampires. Yes, I know about Tor. You can't keep things like that from me...especially since I'm a good friend of your Aunt Morwena! I know your family keeps the witch lore as part of your early education and life, and that makes sense, but your parents and aunt didn't keep you well-rounded with other paranormal beings and their traditions—and idiosyncrasies."

"There is a definite lack of education among witches when it comes to other Breed. Sometimes I feel so inadequate dealing with my team, um, being a part of such a group." I mentally chastised myself for almost slipping, giving away the fact that I am the leader.

"I know about that too, Mags. Why do you think I'm a trusted human? Dale and I used to work for your Aunt Morwena when she was head of the organization. I managed everything for her, and Dale was her driver. We've been doing this since we were newlyweds. I know she asked you to take over for her and all the hard work you put in to make it to the top."

Well, then.

Aunt Morwena certainly could have informed me of this—but I wouldn't hold it against her. I was hardly ever home, and when I was, I tended to hide in my bedroom and catch up on reading and sleep. I had no one to blame but myself; forever the introvert.

"So, what is it about Tor that I am unaware of? Are all vampires jerks or something? Even half-vampires like Tor?"

"I wouldn't describe them in that manner. It's just that vampires covet things. When they decide something is theirs then something happens to challenge this, they become jealous to the extremes and will stake their claim—no pun intended." Estelle chuckled. "Even a crossbreed such as Tor will have an incredible urge to take what they see as theirs and challenge anything in their path from keeping it away from them. Which is why many vampires date in secret if they date at all."

"So he's being aloof. Why?" I asked, perplexed despite Estelle giving suggestions for Tor's behavior.

"Perhaps he doesn't want to show you his jealous side. If he remains distant, you won't see the torment he is going through nor will he have to see your anger for his attitude. I'm not trying to make excuses for him, but a vampire is a funny creature. They live forever—well, they are immortal unless someone manages to do them in. Difficult to be sure, but it can be done as you have seen with what happened last month. Someone like Tor doesn't take dating lightly. It is a major commitment for them, especially seeing as he will outlive you. By centuries."

Now there was a sobering thought. Maybe he wasn't mad at me, but jealous of the time we are wasting, the distractions and occurrences that are keeping us apart. Or maybe, and this was something that gave me pause— maybe Tor no longer wanted to go out with me and doesn't know how to tell me. After all, he must see how mismatched we are. He will outlive me. I'm just a witch. Maybe he needs to look for a lifemate, another vampire who will spend a lifetime with him. Or maybe his intent was never to get too close, and I was supposed to be a fling —reckless, considering I'm the boss, but Tor doesn't know that now, does he?

But Tor needed to realize communication meant everything to me, and while I might not like the jealous tendencies of a vampire, I certainly disliked being shut out by him even more. Plus, I wouldn't invest in this relationship if the lines of communication were down, leaving me guessing and worrying.

Sigh. And everyone wonders why I prefer being a loner!

"Thanks for the talk, Estelle. I appreciate you taking the time in your busy day."

"Busy? *Pshaw!* That's what I have my crew running around like lunatics for. I'm never too busy for you, my dear. Now get ready to have a little talk with your vampire Scot because he's heading this way!"

Turning, I watched a determined-looking Tor slowly making his way toward my table. Each move catlike and sexy, yet he seemed oblivious to the appreciative looks he was garnering from several women he passed. His reddish-brown hair newly shorn, yet still longish as the sunlight made his highlights pop. I wondered if the sun was an issue seeing as his eyes were hidden behind mirrored sunglasses.

Steady girl. This should be good—or not.

Looks like I'm about to deal with a jealous vampire. But even as this thought crossed my mind, another more disturbing one followed suit. What if Tor was so jealous, he removed one of the threats by taking out Levi Patel? Is *he* the one we should be looking at? Is Daniel Grayson innocent? And would he be the next victim if Tor found him before we did?

Suddenly, my headache went from bad to much worse.

CHAPTER 11

Tor took the seat Estelle had vacated and didn't say anything at all. He just watched me organize my table and prepare for any customers that might find me way out here on the edge of nowhere. I wouldn't say I was nervous. But I suddenly felt the need to look over all the paperwork we had on each one of my team members. My lack of caring about those details—most of them I eagerly passed on to Antoine—the central figure who vetted all new hires—had me angered.

Aunt Morwena was backup to Antoine in that department, which left me free to plan our strategy on monster-hunting and focus on the paranormal end of the antique appraisals. What it did not do was make me a good leader—and I had only myself to blame. I should already know everything about Torquil MacDonald. Where he came from, what's in his past, where he worked, who he loved, where his people lived—everything. Instead, I sat here wondering how I could get a message to Antoine and whether I was facing a cold-blooded killer.

My lack of education on other paranormal Breeds ended today. Tonight. I would begin research by reading. Heaven knows I have a mini-library at my disposal in one overcrowded section of my RV. It was time to educate myself in a hurry.

Tor was patient. I will give him that. He sat with his beautifully manicured hands folded on the table and waited with a neutral expression on his handsome face. His hazel eyes with their brown starburst on a light green background remained aloof, yet I could detect sadness in them, and something else—longing.

Yet, despite sensing this, I refused to react, or engage him in conversation.

I had removed my gloves because the humidity was making my hands sweat. I made the motion to pick them up once more when Tor reached out and grabbed my right hand—holding on tightly—as I tried pulling it from his firm grip. The minute our palms touched I was rocked with one image after another coming at me with such intensity I gasped.

Images after image. Tor a child, in his village in Scotland, then a town in North Carolina where he informed me his family moved when he was a pre-teen. School days, first kiss, loss of a pet, loss of his grandmother, all jumbled imagery that slammed into me and caused me to cry out. Only then did he release me.

"You wanted to know me better, pet. Now you do."

My temper flared and I felt violated and raw. "Don't you ever do that to me again. Ever! You have no right to use me in such a way!" I stood and faced him with my hands balled into fists.

"Use you? I could hear your thoughts a mile away. I picked up the change in your scent and knew it tied to me somehow. I felt your concern and worry—and fear. I could not have that, pet. Not fear. What did I ever do to deserve your mistrust?"

I could feel the vibrations of anger pouring off the man I had become so attracted to I couldn't sleep at night without him creeping into my dreams—and knew I was in trouble.

"How can you hear my thoughts? What do you mean you smelled my fear? How can a half-breed vampire pick up so much from a field anyway?" I hoped those glamour spells the witches of Sweet Briar set over the town were in full force and none of the humans just heard me scream that at Tor. I certainly was beyond caring, however, because once my red got up, I was too hot to give a fig!

"Who told you I was half-vampire? My sweet, I am almost *all* vampire. I only have a bit of sorcerer in me, and even that bastard had vampire in him. I might as well be considered full-blooded!" Tor shouted back at me. I guess his dark reddish-brown hair might give him a bit of a temper as well.

"You certainly don't look like a vampire, much, some...not really." Great. I sounded like an imbecile.

"And what is a vampire supposed to look like, huh? Can you tell me? What about a witch? A shifter? Do we all need to look the same?" He was breathing hard which I found hilarious for some reason considering he didn't have many working organs now that I knew he was pretty much a vamp!

"Like Mortimer. Or Valgaard. They look like vampires!" Mortimer and Valgaard were two vampires who came to our aid when we took out the strix. Mortimer is friends with Lily and Adriana and looked like Lurch from the old *The Addams Family* television show.

"Mortimer's people are from Tasmania. Have you seen that lot? He also has ties to Romania. He is as vampire as you can get, and his line is ancient. Valgaard looks like a Visigoth,

a mix of Germanic and Spanish. And what about Caliente, his daughter? Does she look like a vampire? She looks nothing like Mortimer," argued Tor.

He had me there.

"Well, she... she..." Yeah. I had nothing.

"How would you know what a freakin' Visigoth looked like anyway?" I asked crossing my arms on my chest in a defensive move.

Tor just arched one eyebrow at me and gave me such a look of incredulity I gulped. Loudly.

"Tor, how old are you?"

The anger evaporated as quickly as it came, and I sat back down in my chair in a heap of misery. Tor sat across from me again and handed me my gloves. It was such a sweet gesture of understanding that I almost began to cry. Almost. I refused to show weakness—my famous Scottish hot temper would not allow me to appear weak.

"Maggie, I would rather not say just yet. I hoped we could get to know each other better. Form a trust. Move forward in our relationship first. Now, I wonder if we will get that chance."

"I didn't mean to doubt you," I said.

"Yet you went there faster than a mouse on cheese. Let me guess. You worked things out in your head and somehow remembered I am a vampire, realized this appears to be a passion murder—meaning whoever our killer is acted out of hate. We all know love and hate go together. Then you made the connection that a vampire is covetous and jealous by nature and hello, here we are."

Tor wasn't wrong.

Yet sitting here now, staring into those eyes and hearing his voice—and after seeing his life flash before my eyes, I knew he was no killer. Not in that sense anyway. He's killed —heck we all did in this business—but he wasn't a cold-blooded murderer.

"I'm sorry," I squeaked out.

"Nay, I'm sorry, lass. For keeping my distance. I didn't want you to feel the anger and jealousy coming off me and you thinking it was aimed at you. I tried to swallow it and took it out on Johnny."

"What did you do?" I had vision of *Twilight* passing through my mind with vampires battling werewolves and shuddered. "Please tell me you didn't fight!"

"No. I kept him up nights reading Robert Burns aloud in our RV. Drove him mad, it did. Now he refuses to sleep in that tin can and has taken to sleeping on a hammock between two trees in the nearby woods."

I felt the bubbling giggle come up and out of me before I could stop myself, then it turned into full-on laughter.

Tor joined in and in no time we were discussing more ways to torture Johnny while wiping the tears from our faces.

"Did you read him Burns' poems on Scotland and friendship?" I asked between snickers.

"Nay, 'twas all romantic stuff, *Ae Fond Kiss* and *my love is like a red, red rose* and the like."

"Poor Johnny!"

"Aye. He will think of something horrible to get me back. I'm sure of it," Tor chuckled.

"*Ae Fond Kiss*, huh? Yeah...he will definitely make you hurt." I tried to keep it light but noticed the instant Tor went from jovial to serious. I watched as his eyes lowered to my mouth and felt the need to swallow hard again...this time I managed not to. When he leaned forward and brushed the back of his fingers down my cheek, I gasped.

Then he continued his forward momentum until our faces were inches apart.

"Oh, how lovely. Making out in public...*and* in front of children!"

Nathara. Our not-so-friendly neighborhood dark witch came walking up behind my chair and flicked my ear before ruffling Tor's hair. She and I had this love-hate frenemy thing going and right now I did not feel like engaging in any snarky banter. And kids? What did she...oh. When I surveyed the area, I noticed a family at a nearby table selling their wares giving Tor and me surreptitious glances. The two young boys, brothers, by their similar appearance, started making kissy noises. I wanted to die on the spot.

"What do you want, Nathara?" Tor ignored the children and focused on the witch who came to stand on my left.

"I don't want anything. Antoine, however, is needing the both of you to pack up this little experiment and get Maggie over to the main auction group. Something has come up."

"Did he say what it is?" I asked hopefully.

Nathara shrugged then smirked. "No, but even if he did, I wouldn't tell you."

Then she sauntered off back the way she had come from, giving Tor a parting look over her shoulder. Nathara could pull off coquettish looks. Me? Not so much.

"If I had to guess, pet, and my hearing isn't off, they found Daniel Grayson." Tor responded.

Wait. What? Why did I think this wouldn't be good news?

CHAPTER 12

On our way back to the main building that housed our antique troupe, I couldn't help noticing Pandora running off into the woods ahead of us. Had she been spying on me? It looked that way. I mean, she had binoculars and was dressed in subdued clothing— for the crossroads demon, anyway. And if I'm not mistaken, Adriana Dolce was with her. What the heck?

Adriana, you couldn't miss. She had on some kind of weird outfit and was holding a ridiculously large magnifying glass. And despite the heat, she had a neon green knit cap on her head with a sparkly orange pom-pom on top. She looked like a deranged Waldo incapable of hiding or blending in anywhere.

"Tor, did you see that?"

"Yep."

"Care to wager the whys of it?"

"Nope."

Yeah. Neither did I.

"There you are!" Dara came rushing over, scolding me

as if she wasn't in on the plan to stick me out in the middle of nowhere so I'd be a target of sorts.

"Here I am. What's up? Where is Antoine?"

"Antoine is with that nice detective, Brian Chase. They've found Daniel. Or they think he's been sighted. But there is some bad news attached to it. We think Danny attacked Dev Patel, the cousin of Levi. He was picking up his cousin's personal effects and someone jumped him in the alley behind the hospital if you can believe it."

"Oh no! Is he dead? That poor man!"

"No, not dead, but he's out cold and the doctors didn't like his head injury, so they induced a coma. He's bad, but the doctors informed us he will pull through. Detective Chase put 24-hour security around the man because he surely knows who attacked him. Now there is an all-points bulletin out for Daniel Grayson. This has gone from bad to worse."

"This is going to come back and bite Ellie...and me. I just know it."

"Well, speaking of that. That Samantha Geist is here looking for you. Come. Let's go into the office the adminis-trators of this building have set aside for us. She's waiting there with Antoine."

As we walked down the corridor that led to the meeting room, we ran into Lily, Andrea, and Lorcan coming from the opposite direction.

"Lily! Hey, did you hear about Mr. Patel? Dev... Levi's cousin?"

"We just came from the hospital. Andrea found him! She was bringing a delivery of cookies and pastries from her dad's café for the weekly nurses meeting and found him off to the side of the path between the parking deck and the outbuilding that leads to the ER."

"It was horrible," cried Andrea. "I thought he was dead, but then he moaned!"

"He's lucky you found him when you did. Can you imagine if no one came along?" Lily put her arm around her cousin, and I knew Andrea was a mess because she was still trembling.

"Maggie. Good, come in here. Bring your cousin and friends." Antoine poked his head out from one of the rooms and waved us in. When we entered, we found Samantha Geist and Brian Chase, heads together and mumbling over some notes and photographs. Ellie was hovering over Samantha's shoulder and smiled at me when we made eye contact. The worry on her face couldn't be hidden behind her smile.

"We are going to go over some things and this room will offer us some privacy from the police department, the Council, and anyone else we are trying to keep out of the loop," said Antoine.

"Hey! Where did they go? I just saw them!"

"How should I know? I can't see anything. The glare off your pom-pom has blinded me."

"Oh no. Is that my great-grandmother? And Dorie?" Lily groaned and dropped her head to the table just as the two in question came waltzing into the room.

"Ah! Here they are. Good. Looks like we're just in time."

"Why do you have a pom-pom hat on in June?" Lorcan looked shocked, then shook his head holding his hands up. "You know what? Forget I asked."

"You're lucky I am choosing to forget you asked that because I don't have time to spell you, buster." Adriana turned to the room and drew herself up preparing to inform us of something momentous I'm sure, only Antoine didn't seem to have gotten the memo.

"Ladies, sit, please. I have much to discuss and can't be distracted right now."

Adriana closed her mouth with a snap of her teeth, frowned, then took a seat. I could see Lily and her friends release the pent-up breaths they'd been holding and held back a smile. I connected eyes with Pandora who shrugged and grinned evilly.

"Dev Patel will be able to tell us who attacked him once he awakens. Brian has put a guard on his room, and we need to make sure no one tries to get to him. The thing is, Daniel Grayson's vehicle was caught on the hospital cameras leaving the area just after the time the police ascertained Dev was attacked, He looks like our man," Antoine informed the room at large but zeroed in on me.

"Maggie, I need you to be very careful. We have no idea if he is still in the area or left yet."

"I put a call in to his station up in Mystic Valley. They stated he had built up vacation time, so they didn't think it was odd that he took off," said Brian. "I told his supervisor he was a person of interest, just for some questions regarding an ex-girlfriend, and he informed me he'd let us know if Daniel showed back up in Mystic Valley."

"He's so cute when he's acting like a cop," Pandora cooed.

Brian blinked and widened his eyes when Dorie bared her teeth in a smile. "I am a cop."

"So cute."

"Anyway, we'd like to get answers now, but the doctors said it would be a few days before they bring Dev back up from that induced coma. So we have no choice but to sit on our hands for a bit."

"Pooh. We've set a trap. We intend to catch this creep tonight."

"Dorie! What are you talking about? Grandmother,

what does she mean? What have you done?" Lily looked perplexed and irate at the same time, and Lorcan put his hand on her shoulder, calming her instantly. I wondered how it felt to have an empath do their thing like he just did. I bet I wouldn't have so many headaches.

"Oh, now you want to hear what I have to say? Pandora and I have set up a trap. We are going to use your cousin as bait, just like you talked about last night. We will draw the baddie out and he won't be able to escape because I've come up with a spell that will make him unable to leave with Maggie, nor will he be able to stop talking about what he's done if she is close enough to ask him if he killed Levi."

"But Maggie will be in a dangerous position!" Andrea squealed. "She could be injured—or worse!"

"Maggie eats danger for breakfast, lass. Don't you fret," Tor stated, giving me a wink.

"Hang on a minute. If we want to capture Daniel, why don't we just set up a trap at the hospital. We can see if he shows up—which he is wont to do to keep Dev from being able to oust him—and nab him that way? All we need to do is hide in a room we pretend Dev is in, and grab him when he sneaks in," I asked, looking sheepishly at Adriana and Pandora for grandstanding away from their plan.

"Well sure, we can do that, but like this big vamp just said, it could be days before Dev wakes up...what if it isn't your ex?"

"First of all, stop calling him my ex. We dated a long time ago when we were teenagers. Second, who else could it possibly be? I hate to put the blame on me and Ellie, but we probably caused this inadvertently during our last case," I grumbled.

Samantha cleared her throat. "About that. I was able to pull a few strings and shift the focus off Ellie, but if he kills again, or you fail to capture him and he uses some nefarious means to get to Dev, I won't be able to keep The Order from questioning Ellie...and that will mean I need to subdue her in ghost form. This could harm her chances of coming back to this realm."

"Why? What will you do to her?" Lily cried.

"Bind her to me. Compel her to speak and register her as a lost soul. Once that happens and The Order finishes questioning her, I will have no choice but to move her on to her next life. We won't be able to have Adriana find that cure and remove the dark magic allowing her to return to her body."

Samantha looked miserable saying this and Ellie began to twitch. I could see she wanted to flee out the door—or through the walls—and hide. But I suspected nothing my sister could do would keep Samantha from finding her at this point.

"Well, we need to do everything we can to capture Daniel and take the heat off my sister right now!" I demanded.

"I don't think he's our guy. He didn't smell right to me," said Pandora.

"Dorie! Not now! OK?" Lily sighed and gave the demon a scolding look.

"What? I'm serious. I watched Maggie sitting out in left field all day looking all hot and bothered and I saw no less than fifteen guys ogling her. Some of them even came up to her and handed her things!"

"Um, Dorie? I'm an antique appraiser. I was doing appraisals all day," I informed her.

"Yes, but did you smell any of those men? I'm telling you. I picked up a scent that has me thinking we may be barking up the wrong pole."

"Tree."

"What?" Pandora turned to Lily who had her head down on the table and was slightly banging it.

"Barking up the wrong tree."

"I wasn't sitting in a tree. I was on top of that pole thingamajig in the woods."

"The cell tower?" Lorcan asked with incredulity, since the item in question was very tall and dangerous to be near.

"Maybe? I think so. I'm not sure what a cell tower is. But if it's that big structure out back, then yes."

Lily began to groan.

Adriana stood up, adjusting her purse. "We need to leave, Pandora. They don't believe us."

Pandora tilted her head and considered Lily first, then peered at the rest of us.

"Come along. We can go talk to the sheriff and his new deputy. Maybe they will listen."

Lily really began banging her head on the table at this proclamation, and Lorcan had to physically restrain her before she cracked her skull.

"Why?"

"It's OK, hon."

"No, really. Why?"

Pandora and Adriana hadn't been gone a minute when Garrison Black popped his head into the room.

"Oh, I'm sorry. I was looking for Maggie. Hey! Mags...I went to your table to bring you that water, but you weren't there," he scolded.

"Oh, Garrison. I'm so sorry. I got called in here and forgot. Thanks though. I appreciate it." Taking the water from him, I smiled sheepishly, and he returned my grimace with a slight grin.

"I'm going to head back out on the floor. Estelle is in

full dragon mode, and I'm worried about the twins' survival at this rate."

When he left, Johnny came into the room. "Tor! I need you man; we have a line."

Tor got up, albeit reluctantly, and left with Johnny after one last penetrating stare. This time I winked.

"Now, to get back to this setting a trap matter..."

Antoine barely got that out when Bella, Serena, and Sydney came running into the room. It was turning into Grand Central around here!

"There you are! Maggie, we need to talk. Do you know that idiot crossroads demon was watching you all day with a pair of binoculars? We think she's up to something!"

Not again.

"Don't worry about Pandora, and certainly don't let her hear you three accusing her of anything!" I scolded.

"Yeah, well we aren't going to let her get the upper hand this time around. We made a plan," Bella sniffed, placing a box down on the table and pushing it toward Brian. "Here. This is the box Dev Patel was carrying when he got attacked. We were sniffing around the hospital looking for clues and heard an orderly getting ready to hand this over to the police. So we stole it and brought it to you so they couldn't get their hands on it first."

"Who? The police?" asked Brian, scratching his head.

"Yeah! Duh!" said Bella.

"But I am the police!" Brian was starting to sound shrill. "If they had brought it to the police station, I would have gotten it at that time."

"Yeah, but not before the police pored over everything and ruined the scent."

What is it with elementals and demons and smelling things?

"Aha! I knew I smelled our perp! Either it's one of these three or they have something that belongs to our killer on them!" Pandora popped back into the room with Adriana hot on her heels.

"Whoa." Serena and Sydney made exactly the same sound when they beheld Adriana. And who could blame them?

"Why is that old witch dressed like that?" Serena was bold enough to ask.

"Old? I will have you know..."

"Grandmother! Enough. We don't have time for any of this!" Lily shouted.

Pandora was sniffing the box while the three women on my team started in with the growling again.

Antoine, sensing trouble was afoot, instructed Bella, Serena, and Sydney to head back to work—and leave the box for Brian to examine—with thanks for their help and suggestions.

It didn't fool the three that they were being dismissed, so they scowled and strutted out of the room with their heads held high. "You'll see."

Pandora continued to sniff around the room, looking confused. "This box smells funny, but so does the room in general."

"Maybe Lorcan passed wind," suggested Adriana.

"Hey!"

"It could happen."

"Can we please figure out what we intend to do?" I asked, the exasperation evident in my voice.

"You can plan all you want. Dorie and I will solve this thing because no one wants to listen to us. Come on Pandora. Let's go catch us a killer!" Adriana once again swept out of the room with a sniffing Dorie. Maybe now things would settle down and we'd actually come up with the plan.

How come I had a troublesome feeling Adriana and Pandora might be correct?

CHAPTER 13

We spent a few more minutes coming up with a plan, and it was decided that a combo of the two ideas might work out. We would put Antoine and Tor as trackers on me as I made my way to the hospital as a Goodwill ambassador, visiting Dev Patel with Lily. Daniel had no idea we were magical, so two women out late wandering around the hospital grounds had to be something he'd not pass up on—if he was still around—and the killer. No human would detect a pair of vampires watching.

Then Sven would lie in wait in the hospital room we would loudly be discussing as Dev's, in the hopes that he'd try something and could be captured there. Sven was a shifter and told us he'd turn into a piece of medical equipment while a dummy remained in the hospital bed. Hopefully, if Daniel slipped past us, or didn't come after us, he'd go after Dev.

I honestly didn't think Daniel would make a move on me. Why would he? Dev was the threat. We had no proof Daniel was the killer and unless he did something rash, everything was circumstantial. Of course, we had ways of turning circumstantial into reality and Daniel would then be toast.

I was to meet Lily at her home, then we'd drive over in her Jeep. It was a short walk from the fairgrounds to there, and I kind of hoped Danny would pop out at me and go "boo" so I could flatten him. The quandary was whether or not he was under such an influence from Ellie that he'd kill to have me as his own. That's where things would get sticky for us and mean heaps of trouble for my sister.

Samantha was hovering around the square, also hidden, as the representative making sure we didn't do something to Daniel untoward because, yeah—protect Ellie!

"Here goes nothing." I began my walk from the now-empty fairgrounds. Everything had wound down for the evening and most people were at home watching television or having a late dinner.

I walked to the square, peering around nervously to see if I could find where Samantha was sequestered. I couldn't detect her anywhere. Turning down south Main, I went a block to Lily's street and turned left. She met me on the corner already in her Jeep and I climbed in.

"Any sign of anything?" she asked.

"Nope. It's another peaceful night in Sweet Briar."

"Heh. Try telling that to my great-grandfather. Adriana's parents came over from Italy a few weeks back and still haven't left. He's going crazy with his unwanted houseguests! I mean, Lou and Lizzie are sweet, and my great uncle Rudy is a hoot, but they tend to wear you out to the point of madness!" Lily stated.

"Lou and Lizzie?"

"They refuse to have me call them great-great anything!"

We made our way to the hospital on the north side of town just before you reached the town limits and it turned rural. Lily parked in the outside lot, avoiding the parking deck so we'd be forced to walk quite a distance to get into the hospital. Our hope was that if Daniel was following us, he'd make a move.

"So, Dev is in Room 203? It was nice of the nurse to let us know and allow us to visit him since he's showing signs of waking up." I said to Lily a bit loudly.

"Yes. I'm glad he's in Room 203. It's much better than having to walk all the way to the other side of the hospital."

We slowly made our way across the parking lot and something just didn't feel right. I couldn't put my finger on it, but something was off. Just before we reached the last row of cars before we arrived at the entrance, Lily's phone went off. "It's Lorcan. Let me grab this."

"Sure."

Lily walked a few feet away from me and answered her call. I could hear a one-sided conversation that had me thinking whatever was being said on the other side of that call was way more exciting than what we were facing. I looked up and saw Sven walking out toward us and knew either Daniel had been caught or he was elsewhere.

"OK, thanks Lorcan."

Lily hung up and turned back to me. By the time she did this, Sven was at our side.

"That was Lorcan. He said Brian called him. They found Daniel. He was passed out drunk in his car and they have him down at the station waiting for him to sleep it off."

"Antoine called to inform me. I guess this was an elaborate ruse that didn't need to play out. Ah, well. I can drive

Maggie back to the fairground unless you plan on going to the station."

Lily looked at me to see what I'd say, but I suddenly wanted nothing more than to head back to my RV, curl up with Bob, and get an early night to be ready for whatever tomorrow would bring.

"OK, I will see you tomorrow, Maggie. We will figure it out. Hopefully, Daniel will clear up some things—and admit to murder—so we can avoid Ellie getting into trouble. Where is she anyway?"

"That's a very good question. Does anyone have Samantha's number? I'm worried she will run off with Ellie and I will never see her again!"

"I'll call her and find out what's up...then text you. Go get some sleep." Lily said goodbye to Sven who ushered me to his vehicle, and we turned back around toward the fairgrounds and our RVs.

"Are you heading straight back to the fairgrounds, Sven?" I asked.

"I was going to head to the police to nose around and meet up with Antoine and Tor. Do you want to come?"

I thought about it for half a second but realized my worry for Ellie was pronounced. I needed to find out if she was safe back at our RV or if I needed to confront Samantha. I also needed something to eat and drink or I would pass out.

"Just take me back to the fairgrounds so I can get some rest. I have a feeling tomorrow will be even crazier than today."

Sven drove me home and went so far as to make sure I reached my RV. I went up the steps, only to be greeted by an irate Bob, desperate for food and over this trip to Georgia. Bob, like me, preferred being on the road! Looking around, I was disappointed to realize Ellie was not where I hoped, and

I began to fret. I fed Bob, giving him extra kibble and hugs then went to wash the spoon in the sink. Taking off my gloves, I washed off the spoon and a few other items I'd left until later, then dried my hands and glanced out the window.

That's when I saw a figure near our tents—or more specifically, my tent, which was cordoned off by police tape. What's more, they had a pumpkin similar to the one I'd found poor Levi Patel's head stuffed in, and I froze.

Now, I'm not some idiot character in a movie that suddenly has an urge to head out and investigate for herself, winding up in the clutches of the bad guy. Nor would I cower in my RV and pretend danger wouldn't come for me only to get trapped inside. Instead, I grabbed my cell phone and purse, speed-dialed Antoine while I picked up Bob and tossed him in the tiny bathroom, then snuck outside, creeping around the side of my RV and rushing into the wood line so I had a better vantage point.

"Maggie!"

"Shh, Antoine. I'm outside in the woods beside our RVs. Where is everyone?"

"Maggie, what's wrong?"

"I just saw someone walking around our tents...and the figure was carrying a pumpkin as big as the one Levi Patel had," I whispered furiously.

"OK, stay on the line with me. I'm sending Tor—he's right here. Also, Johnny should be coming your way. Tor is texting him," Antoine informed me, and I could hear him barking orders at the police station and wondered who he was ordering around.

"I want to nab this guy, Antoine. I just need some backup."

"I know you do, Mags. Hold tight."

Sighing internally, I opened my tote and began

fumbling around looking for chocolate or something to munch on while I waited. That's when my hand grabbed the water bottle Garrison had handed me earlier and everything in my world shifted, and I was thrust into the very recent past.

"You never should have approached Margaret. She is a lady and would never be with someone like you!"

"I'm sorry, but I do not know who you are? Why are you in here?" Levi Patel looked frightened and had dropped the large pumpkin which rested by his feet. "Please, let me go. I just came to leave an apology note and will not bother Maggie again."

"Margaret! Her name is Margaret!" I could feel the spittle coming out of Garrison's mouth and knew I was seeing events as they happened through his eyes. The eyes of a madman and the person who killed Levi Patel. I tried to will myself back to the present but remained stuck in my psychic impression.

"Please. I promise I will go away. This is a misunderstanding. My cousin tells me I forever get mixed messages from women and fixate on them. But it was harmless. I only wanted to take her out on a date...see where it led."

"See where it led? You filthy pig. Margaret is mine. I've watched her for years now and waited until I had enough money tucked away to run off with her and start our life together. She is mine, don't you understand? Mine! You don't know things about her and her people, but I do. And I know how to cure her of it!"

"I don't understand?" Levi was looking everywhere for an escape from this lunatic, but when the realization he would either have to fight his way out or die trying to escape hit, the poor man began to blubber. "Please don't kill me."

"Oh, but you are already dead. Dead and no longer a threat to my happiness."

"Margaret. It's time to let that go. Stand up, my dear."

I heard the voice, and my blood ran cold as I flew backward into the present and looked up to see Garrison Black standing over me holding a rope. I could hear Bob in my RV howling and spitting and wondered if I could drop this lunatic and make a run for it. But coming out of my psychic magic always left me groggy and disoriented—and Garrison knew it. He was a trusted human after all.

"I don't understand," I managed to get out.

"You're just a woman. Of course you don't." I felt a tiny prick of a needle and tried to pull away only I couldn't move quickly enough. I could feel whatever horrible medicine Garrison was using on me spread through my veins. And I began to dry heave in reaction.

"Now stand up. That's my dear. Let's head off toward my car. We are going far away where you can be lady of my manor, and I will rule your world with a firm hand but justly—as long as you obey."

My legs obviously worked as I was yanked upright and pushed to move across the clearing in the woods and out into the open as we began to walk across the fairground. Thoughts raced through my mind, and I felt hollowed-out and spacey. I knew help was nearby because Antoine said Tor was coming. And Johnny. And...

"Quickly, now. Quickly. That's right. Look at how nice and empty the park is. Everyone is over at the garage to get a piece of that stupid cop you dated. Shame on you, Margaret. I will have to punish you for that mistake."

We reached a huge grey sedan that had rental plates on it, and I began to freak out. Where were my friends? My family?

Garrison opened the door and settled me into the front

seat then ran around and hopped in his side. Turning on the engine, I could hear the tires rotate even as I noticed a figure rushing across the grounds at top speed. Tor!

I felt my magic trying to kick on, but it kept fizzling out even as my mind began to wander and the nausea became intense.

"Going to be sick."

"Don't you even dare, sweetness. Or you'll feel my hands upon you sooner than I planned. I cannot wait to punish and train you—break you, then keep you properly trained and obedient. We will have such a wonderful life."

The car was racing away, and my head leaned on the cool window as I stared out into the darkness, the road whisking by at top speed, and I willed myself to stay coherent. I was a strong witch and began to reject whatever human medicine he'd stuck into me. I pictured the droplet of medicine oozing out my pores and felt myself go into a cold sweat. That's right. I flexed one hand, keeping it hidden as I waited for my body to mend itself and become whole again.

I didn't even get halfway there, nor did Garrison reach the edge of the town of Sweet Briar, when we felt something slam into the car that careened us off the roadway and down a ditch where we came to a rolling stop, winding upside down in a dizzying mess of crushed metal and glass.

Garrison moaned next to me as I peered out, blearily trying to make out any formation to see what we'd hit—or hit us rather! That's when I saw a pair of high-heeled stiletto shoes standing just outside my window, then the top of Pandora's head as she leaned down to peer into my window.

"Heya, girlie! Everything OK?"

I guess the events and medicine, lack of food and drink

finally caught up to me, because my eyes rolled back into my head, and I gave myself up to oblivion.

My last thought was, *Gee, I hope Dorie was here to claim my soul.*

"Dorie, get out of the way! I think I hit that car with way too much magic. Maggie might be in trouble!" Lily cried.

Oh, OK then, my own cousin tried to kill me.

I could hear a whistling sound and lost my sense of smell.

Then everything faded to black.

CHAPTER 14

"There she is! Hey, Mags! How do you feel?"

I opened my eyes to a dimly lit hospital room and found my sister Ellie gazing down at me with a broad smile across her face. Lily was next to her, and Pandora was just behind them. She gave me a jaunty little salute as I made to sit up.

"Oh, wow. Kill me now."

"Hadn't you had enough of that last night, kiddo?" Adriana Dolce blinked over at me as I slightly turned my head in her direction.

"What happened?"

"What happened? What happened is we caught your bad guy while the rest of these nincompoops chased the wrong man hither and yon!" sniffed Adriana. "We tried to tell you, but no one listened to Pandora and me. Oh, no. We had to be the heroes while everyone came scrambling across the fairground too late to do much of anything but look stupid."

"Granny, enough. She is not going to let us hear the

end of this one. I swear." Lily looked distressed and her frown deepened when Pandora began to speak.

"Hey. I told you I smelled something off. It took me a minute to realize the scent I'd picked up outside while watching people coming and going from Maggie's table matched the scent I smelled in the office you were all sitting in. Then I tracked it to that nasty Garrison Black. I was all set to blast the car off the road, but Lily here, beat me to it." Pandora gave a little chuckle and pointed at Lily. "Of course, this one used too much power in her rush to save the day and lifted your car clear in the air then dropped you down until you rolled to that stop, so hooray for seatbelts!"

"I'm so sorry Maggie! I got a bit ambitious." Lily tried to apologize but I wouldn't hear a thing about it.

"Don't you dare. You saved me Lily. OK, you went about it in a unique and unusual way but stop that car—and the evil asshat—you did!" I tried to smile but my face still felt frozen and I had a trickle of fear course through me that something might be wrong with it. I went to place my hand on my face and groaned when even that was too much effort.

"Steady girl. You had a nasty ride, and the clerics pumped a lot of medicine in you to clear out whatever Black jabbed you with," Antoine uttered softly. I could hear his voice but dared not turn in his direction. The nausea that had been ever-present decided to jumble my tummy, turning me all shades of green. I was sure of it.

"Uh-oh, better call the nurse. I think this one is about to blow!" cried Pandora.

Gee, do you think?

IT TOOK three more days of recuperating back at Lily's house to feel like my old self again. Surprisingly, I awoke on the second day to find Bob curled up on one side of me with Wicked on the other. Sometime during my recuperation, both felines decided they could be friendly toward one another and now the purring was an intense stereo effect that kept lulling me back to sleep.

But on day three, I'd had enough pampering, and my usual healthy appetite came back with a vengeance.

I was downstairs raiding the kitchen when Lily found me with a chicken leg in one hand and a Yoo-hoo in the other.

"I like your food offerings. I may just stay here, move in, and become a fixture like one of your ghosts. Heck, Ellie can join them...it will be a party!"

"Someone is feeling better!" Lily smiled, then sobered quickly. "Listen, about my errant magic..."

"Lily, stop. I don't want or need you to apologize to me. You did awesome. OK, so it went a little wonky. But wow...if I'm remembering correctly, it was like a Disney fireworks show mixed with a tsunami of epic proportions. And you managed to not kill me in the process. I see that as a huge success in the magic department."

"But I..."

"But nothing! Where was my highly trained team? By some miracle, you and Pandora and even Adriana did what a skilled tactical team of paranormals failed to do. OK, they had one heck of a red herring with Danny out there. What was his excuse anyway? Why was he skulking around trying to avoid detection?"

"He gave us some line about wanting to apologize to you before anyone forced him to leave town. Dev Patel woke up and identified Garrison as his assailant. There was nothing holding Danny here, and he took off like a hornet after a hound dog. Ellie said her magic finally wore off and he seemed surprised to find himself down here looking for you...so that means she is safe from Samantha and The Order for now. Although Sam did say she'd help Adriana craft that potion when the time came. She's creepy but I kind of like her."

I nodded in agreement and began gnawing on my chicken leg with abandon.

"Where is everyone?" I asked between mouthfuls.

"Closing down the show, wrapping up things, and getting you ready to hit the road once more. Where are you heading next?" Lily asked, and got herself a Yoo-hoo, hip butting me out of the way of the open fridge.

"We're heading down through Atlanta, then winding our way to Charleston, South Carolina for a long weekend. I wish we could stay longer. This turned into a mess in a hurry, and we didn't get time to properly visit."

"You have to come back...or I need to make time to visit when you are in Mystic Valley again." Lily replied.

Oh, I'd like that.

"Estelle cleaned our Garrison's RV and found a warped shrine to you set up in there—beyond disturbing. Apparently he's been going down his road of insanity slowly over the last few years and fixated on you for one reason or another. I just can't believe he thought he could kidnap a witch," said Lily.

"I would have tanned his hide the minute that medicine wore off. Sometimes I get so tired of all the evil out there, but if I didn't do what I do with this crew of mine, the world would be a heck of a lot worse."

"I know it. Trust me."

I thought about what Lily had just been through, retrieving her dad and killing the evil witch that held him prisoner for twenty-one years.

"Have you heard from your parents?" I asked her.

"No. Not that I expect to. Dad is going to need some major help getting over the horrors of the last twenty years and both he and Adelaide will need counseling, I'm sure. It's going to be a tough road for them both."

"I suspect they will make it though," I offered with a smile.

Why did evil need to be among us was one of those questions that would keep me up nights, but I guess without the bad we wouldn't appreciate the good or some such.

Speaking of evil...

"Where does Adriana stand with that reversal spell for Ellie?"

"Ugh, only that it will take months to prepare once we find the right parchment in that bloody library again." Lily noticed my look of alarm and softened her voice. "It's a long story and even longer trek, but fear not. We will find that spell and start working on it."

"Is that? Oh...gave me some of that chocolate cake, please!"

Lily brought the wonderful treat out of the fridge just as Pandora walked in with Ellie trailing behind her.

"And we have a huge compound with several houses, but what's even better is constantly being on the road and fighting all these evil beings that need to be eradicated. We are usually much better at this wort of thing, but with Bella, Serena, and Sydney distracted by you, Tor in a tither over Mags here, and everyone else on high alert but looking at the wrong suspect, we didn't show our best side to you guys!"

Gee, thanks, Ellie.

"I know! You should come visit us sometime! Maybe

we can go shopping like you suggested. Maggie does need some new duds."

Wait, what? No!

"That sounds like fun. If only to spend some time torturing the succubi, and bringing that elemental to tears. It will be a hoot." Pandora reached over and stuck her finger into the cake then licked it.

Speaking of boys in a tither. You should have seen your little dumpling when he witnessed you being forced into that joker's car! Why didn't you inform me he was all vamp and just a tad something else?" Dorie chuckled. "Although I thought so once I got a good sniff of him!"

"What is it with you and sniffing?" Lily argued.

"It's a thing! What can I say? It's worked for eons now and my nose never fails me."

I was too distracted by what Pandora said to pay much attention to anything else the women were bantering about. I wished I could have seen Tor in full freak-out vampire mode. Did that make me shallow? Probably a little, but the girlie part of me wanted to squeal...the rational part wanted to make sure he was OK.

"Estelle is in a tither over this entire Garrison thing." Ellie stated. "She put a call in to Aunt Morwena and demanded we go through all the humans in our troupe and re-vet them for "soundness" as she called it."

"That man was delusional," said Lily.

"Was?" I hadn't thought about his outcome in all this and turned to Ellie who had an evil little smile on her face. Uh-oh.

"Yes, was. After we got you out and took him to the hospital, he tried to escape by crawling out the window...from the fourth floor. He almost made it too, but Samantha appeared next to him on the ledge and scared him something awful. We're not sure exactly what happened, but the next thing anyone heard, he plunged four stories to his death...and Sam made sure to take his soul off to wherever it is she takes them," Ellie finished dramatically.

"Oh, sugar. That's not what I heard," said Dorie. "For the first time in that uptight chick's long life, I think she looked the other way and had a demon take his soul for a spell. Old Garrison Black is in a very, very bad place right about now...and it serves him right!"

"Are you sure, Pandora?" Lily asked with a shocked look on her face.

"But of course! Who do you think she called to escort him to his just reward?"

Yikes! Well, I for one wouldn't mourn that idiot, but still!

CHAPTER 15

"We're heading out of Georgia, and I don't really want to leave!"

"Ellie, if you don't stop singing I am going to strangle you!"

"I'd like to see you try!"

She has a point.

"Well, I really don't want to leave. I'm going to miss Dorie. I think she and I truly are kindred spirits, destined to be fast friends. She's the sister I've always wanted!"

"Hey!"

"Just kidding, sis. But really. I kind of invited her to join us in Mystic Valley. I hope she takes me up on it."

Bella began to growl.

"You mean come for a visit, right? Ellie?"

"Yeah. Of course. Yes...a visit. I hope she comes up someday. She makes me laugh."

And Ellie needs more laughter in her life, so I couldn't begrudge her that.

I think.

Things quickly got back to normal—or as normal as the Mystic Antiques and Uniques Caravan could ever hope to be. I dared not jinx myself and hoped our next stop would be anything short of interesting. Peaceful? What's that?

Bella, Serena, and Sydney growled at Dorie the entire time we were saying our goodbyes. I really hope Pandora forgets about her promise to Ellie, I don't think Mystic Valley, North Carolina could survive such a visit.

Nathara managed to snag a ride with Johnny and Tor and was slithering around them like a snake. I knew she and I were going to come to blows soon. Whether or not they'd be magical, or we'd use fists and bite like humans, would be a matter of contention. Personally, I wanted to punch her.

Tor was back to being sullen and I think his pride got hurt that he couldn't swoop in and save the day. I had Bella with me, and she was driving while I read a book on vampire lore and traditions that I found in my tiny library. I needed to figure out all I could about the man I hoped to date sometime before the next incident fell on our doorstep.

"Put on the radio—a metal station. I want to test out my vocal cords," Ellie began playing air guitar all over the RV and Bob took a few swipes at her every time she passed. Of course, his little kitty paw went right through her!

"Bella if you touch that radio dial, I will personally rip you a new one," I threatened.

"Stop being such a sourpuss. It's better than having her ask us endless questions." *She* had a point.

"OK, so this next stop..." began Bella, and I went to stop her from cursing us by saying it had to be better than our last few trips. "No! I wasn't going to say anything to jinx us! What I was going to say was, did you have time to get any neat stuff? Did any paranormals come to your table?"

"Not a one."

"Well, I did. A really interesting man came up to me and sold me a few items. I have a new Ouija board, an old clock, and a weird-looking lantern or maybe it's a fancy lamp!"

"Just please tell me you haven't rubbed it and we'll be good."

"Um..."

THANK YOU FOR READING! There is only ONE way I am ever going to overtake Nora Roberts and become the next Queen of Paranormal Mystery, Romance and Fantasy—and I can't do it alone. I need your reviews! Won't you please help me achieve my goals? Reviews mean everything to an author, it allows others who may not have heard of me yet take a chance on one of my tales. I hope you consider taking the time to write one for me—and I *thank* you!

I hope you loved meeting Maggie, Ellie, and the rest of the characters. The next book in the Fortune-Telling Twins series is A Djinn and Tonic. A mysterious lamp is left behind by one of Maggie's clients, and when Bella rubs it on a whim, she just may have let a genie out—a very dangerous genie—who has an alcohol problem and intends to go on a bender to beat all benders! One that leads to murder and a mystery decades in the making!

CLICK HERE TO READ A DJINN AND TONIC NOW>

And if you enjoyed Fire and Earth, Sisters at Birth you'll love reading about Maggie and Ellie's cousin, Lily Sweet, a naïve dark witch who discovers her powers and reunites with a family she never knew while coming to terms with her topsy-turvy magical ability. Home Sweet Witch is Book 1 of The Lily Sweet Mysteries and is FREE on Kindle Unlimited!

"Excellent."

- Butterfly & Birch Reviews.

I'd appreciate your help in spreading the word, including telling friends and family. Reviews help readers find books! Please leave a review on your favorite book site.

You can also join my Facebook Group: Author Bettina M. Johnson's Team Wicked for exclusive giveaways and sneak peeks of future books—and just plain silliness!

SIGN UP FOR BETTINA M. JOHNSON'S NEWSLETTER: http://eepurl.com/gZKo51

Continue on for a short excerpt from A Djinn and Tonic…

A Djinn and Tonic

"I DON'T CARE what you say, I think we have a ghost!" Nathara shrieked, slamming out of my RV and storming off into the night.

"Does the woman not know about Ellie? Of course, we have a ghost!" Bella chuckled.

"I don't think Nathara means Ellie's type. She has been claiming a ghost or a pixie must be running loose in our troupe because things of hers keep getting moved and she is convinced a pervert has been going through her underwear drawer," I sighed in resignation.

"A pixie? Didn't we have one after the trip to Knoxville?"

"Yes! And don't remind me. Y'all thought it was hilarious tossing him in my RV and the darn thing lived with me for weeks before I found a mellow band of them living at a gas station on the way to Georgia and tossed him out the window as we left. I hope they didn't skewer him. He was a nice little bugger—for a pixie."

My traveling group of antique appraisers and dealers, Mystic Antiques and Uniques Caravan was on the road through Mount Pleasant, South Carolina. We had just come from an uneventful three days in Summerville, South Carolina and now we were down the road and up the coast, our destination being Murrells Inlet, a coastal town between Charleston and Myrtle Beach.

We would be there for an entire week, partially to play and partially to work our deals and make some serious money. Charleston was always a great moneymaker for us because it was the queen city for antiques of all shapes and sizes. Antiquing was a lifestyle in Charleston, and we always had the best time when we were there.

"Well, I am glad we are staying on the coast...the last time we were stuck in Goose Creek or was it Moncks Corner? Anyway, it's nowhere near as nice as being on a beach!" Bella stated emphatically.

I had to agree.

I adored being anywhere along the Carolina or Georgia coast, and even down into Florida, although that state was bursting at the seams with people everywhere thanks to The Mouse!

"This time we are based right on the beach with the ocean behind us and are a couple of miles away from Brooklawn Gardens. This time I want to visit those gardens. I've heard the sculptures are incredible!" I gushed.

I've heard the place is haunted," said Ellie, popping in. "Antoine said we are ready to roll. Nathara has snuck back in with Tor and Johnny again. I think she keeps offering them a threesome, and so far, they've resisted her charms. Do you want me to go into invisible mode and make sure Tor stays an honest man?"

My sister Ellie is the aforementioned ghost, although we are hoping to rectify that situation soon if my cousin in Georgia and her great-grandmother can find the spell to reverse the dark magic that turned her. We found out Ellie will always be walking halfway in both worlds since whoever turned her did so by making her a revenant—and once a revenant always a revenant. They can have a solid body but can go into ghost mode in an instant. Ellie is glad she will get her body back someday, but I know she's depressed about the other part of it.

"I don't want to have that kind of relationship. I either trust him or I don't."

"You're cute, Mags. Never lose that innocent streak of yours," Bella laughed.

I'm Maggie Fortune. Head of a paranormal group of monster-hunting operatives and daughter of the biggest antique dealer in North Carolina, if not the United States. Yes, I said monster-hunters. We are a ragtag group of witches, vampires, shifters, werewolves, and more, that protected humans and weaker paranormals from evil asshats that want to ruin, destroy, maim, kill, and dominate anyone and everyone. And let me tell you...we get the job done.

Although right now? We just wanted a few days of rest, relaxation, and seafood.

Lots and lots of seafood.

With our track record as of late, I just hoped we'd get some!

SOCIAL MEDIA LINKS

I write in my own style that may not be everyone's cup of tea—so if you enjoy my characters and humor, my plots, how the storyline is developing, etc. and are eagerly antici-pating the next in the series, be aware that I am just as excited as you are—I've found someone who thinks my story ideas are neat! That is thrilling for any writer to know (or it should be). THANK YOU!

Visit my official website to receive updates, find out about special offers and new releases, or read my blog about writing and farm life - complete with photos - you might even catch me mowing my ten acres (seriously): http://www.bettinamjohnson.net

For more information or to contact me:
author@bettinamjohnson.net

For even more (if you just can't enough of me) follow my
Social Media Links

Mailing List - https://bit.ly/2BvQXmP
BookBub - https://bit.ly/2Epejwj
Goodreads - https://bit.ly/3aTejQW
Author Page - Amazon - https://amzn.to/3lj7L2L
Instagram - https://bit.ly/2QpZa01
TikTok - https://bit.ly/2PQa6Hg
MeWe - https://bit.ly/36A2RcM
Facebook - https://bit.ly/3gOaFZY
Twitter: https://bit.ly/3jahMgY
YouTube - https://bit.ly/2Stvy2X

ABOUT THE AUTHOR

I always knew I wanted to write. As a kid, way before the technology age had hit, I'd be stuck in the car with the folks as we drove from our home on Staten Island, NY, where I was born and raised, to our family property in the Catskill Mountains. To drive away boredom, I would sit, staring out the window, and create adventures of daring thieves riding horseback along the road, trying to escape the law. Other times I'd imagine a wild girl riding her unicorn into battle (I had a vivid imagination - we didn't have video games yet!).

As the years passed, I'd start writing a book, then stop, then start again only to let life get in the way, until one day I had an epiphany—a kick in the pants moment. If I waited any longer, all those wonderful characters in my head would never have their stories told, and that made me sad. So, I treated writing as my career. Once I started, it became apparent nothing would ever stop me again. YOU, dear reader, are stuck with me until I go off to that great library in the sky...or wherever writers go when they crumble to dust in front of their typewriters (or laptops...whatever!).

I live in the North Georgia mountains on what I like to call a farm, with my husband and almost adult kids, a Cairn Terrier, a bunch of cats, and fish. Occasionally other critters show up to keep things exciting.

BOOKS BY BETTINA M. JOHNSON

The Lily Sweet Mysteries:

Home Sweet Witch
Witch Way is Up?
How To Train Your Witch
Sweet Home Liliana
Witch Way Did He Go?
Revenge is Sweet, Witch
Witch and Peace
The Sweet Spell of Success
I Spell Trouble (Coming Soon)

The Fortune-Telling Twins Mysteries:

A Tale of Two Sisters
Double Toil and Trouble
Fire and Earth, Sisters at Birth
Kindred Spirits
A Djinn and Tonic (Coming Soon)

Made in United States
North Haven, CT
18 October 2022

25609357R00082